ABOUT THE AUTHOR

DAR   e still
arned
child,
nd he
rly to
n his
a part
place

Sugar

the
Keeps

gst...
amily
oking
seller

make
Keeps

D0227385

*...life must be understood backwards. But...
it must be lived forwards*

Sören Kierkegaard, 1843

WHERE
MERMAIDS
SING

Also by Brian Keaney

Balloon House
Bitter Fruit
Falling for Joshua
Family Secrets
The Private Life of Georgia Brown

ORCHARD BOOKS
96 Leonard Street, London EC2A 4XD
Orchard Books Australia
32/45-51 Huntley Street, Alexandria, NSW 2015
First published in Great Britain in 2004
A PAPERBACK ORIGINAL
Text © Brian Keaney 2004
The right of Brian Keaney to be identified as the author of this
work has been asserted by him in accordance with the Copyright,
Designs and Patents Act, 1988.
A CIP catalogue record for this book is
available from the British Library.
1 84362 419 2
1 3 5 7 9 10 8 6 4 2
Printed in Great Britain

WHERE
MERMAIDS
SING

BRIAN KEANEY

ORCHARD BOOKS

A young woman drives along an empty road in Cornwall one evening in spring. She is in her early twenties, slim with light brown hair and pleasant features. There is nothing very remarkable about her appearance except for her eyes, which are a very pale blue. Although her gaze is focused on the road ahead, there is a distant look on her face that suggests she is locked in her own thoughts and not really listening to the chatter of the little girl who is strapped into the seat behind her.

The girl is about three years old with the same pale blue eyes as her mother. She wants to know whether they are there yet, because it seems to her that they have been driving forever. When her mother makes no reply, the little girl repeats her question more forcefully, emphasising each of the words in turn. 'Are we nearly there yet?' she yells.

'Yes, we are,' the young woman replies, 'but please don't shout.'

She has turned into a large, empty car park, which is no more than a grassless field. Now, she turns off the engine and helps the little girl clamber out of the back seat.

The little girl looks about her with a dissatisfied air.

'Where's the sea?' she demands.

'It's not far,' her mother tells her, as she struggles to button the little girl into a coat and hood.

'I don't want my hood,' the little girl says, pulling it back down again.

'You'll be cold,' warns her mother.

'No, I won't.'

The young woman decides not to pursue the matter further. Instead, she takes her daughter by the hand and together they walk out of the car park and follow a path that leads across some scrubby grass. Large white birds wheel above them, letting out harsh cries quite unlike anything the little girl has heard before. 'What birds are they?' she asks.

'Seagulls,' her mother replies and the little girl twists her head round to stare at them.

'Look!' her woman announces. They have come out behind a wall built of huge concrete blocks that overlooks the sea. The young woman bends down and picks up the little girl so that she can see over the wall. The two of them stare out at water the colour of beaten metal. A path of gold runs across the waves towards the setting sun.

'Is this the special place?' the little girl asks.

The young woman nods. 'That's right.'

'Why is it special?'

'Because this is where I stopped being a child.'

The little girl looks puzzled. 'How?' she asks.

Her mother smiles sadly. 'I just closed my eyes and wished,' she says.

'Did it work?'

'Yes, but not in the way I meant it to.'

1

When things are going well, you don't bother taking stock of what's going on around you, you just get on with it. You get up every morning, dress yourself and walk out into the world with no idea what you're letting yourself in for, perfectly content that you'll be able to deal with whatever comes your way. It doesn't occur to you that this might be the day you'll look back on afterwards and say, that was when it all started.

Certainly Alice didn't expect double English on Friday morning to be anything out of the ordinary. She had no idea that Mr Carmody, her English teacher, would be the one to light the fuse that would burn quietly but steadily through the coming months until it finally triggered an explosion big enough to blow away everything she had become familiar with.

It began with Mr Carmody's announcement. As part of their English course, they would have to produce a number of pieces of creative writing. 'And they have to be really good,' he added, 'because they count towards your exam mark at the end of the year.'

Alice couldn't really get worked up about what was going to happen at the end of the year. It seemed a lifetime away. But what Mr Carmody had to say next *did* make her sit up and take notice. In fact, it made the whole class pay attention.

'This year, the English Department will be organising a trip to Cornwall,' he told them. 'Our hope is that this visit will provide inspiration for some wonderful pieces of writing. Those who take part will stay in a hostel very close to the sea. You'll explore the local area, walk along the beaches and the coastal path, try a bit of rock climbing and then write about your experiences.

Jasmine, who was sitting next to Alice, put her hand up. 'When is it?' she asked.

'The third week in October,' Mr Carmody said, to Alice's immediate dismay. 'I've got some letters about it here. Perhaps you'd like to hand them round?'

Jasmine took the bundle of letters and began distributing them to the other students. Alice seized her copy and immediately checked the date. She discovered, with great disappointment, that it was just as she had suspected. The trip would take place during the week of her sixteenth birthday. That was so annoying! She glanced up to see what the rest of the class were making of the letter but they were all still busily studying the details. Alice felt so frustrated she wanted to bang on the table with her fist. She had been counting on holding a party but now she felt sure there would be no one to invite because everyone would want to go on the trip.

'This looks good,' Jasmine said.

'It's the week of my birthday,' Alice told her.

'That's a pity,' Jasmine replied. 'Still, you can always celebrate when you come back.'

'I suppose so,' Alice agreed, though it didn't sound like a very satisfactory solution.

'Obviously, you'll have to discuss this with your parents,' Mr Carmody went on, 'but who thinks they might be interested in going?'

Everyone in the class put their hands up, even Alice.

That evening, Alice and her friends sat around the table in the garden of The Eagle talking about the trip. Going to the pub with a group of friends on Friday evenings was something she'd started doing recently. In the past, the students in her year had divided themselves up into twos and threes. For the most part, girls had been friends with girls and boys with boys. But recently a change had taken place. Instead of little clusters of individuals, there was suddenly a larger group of girls and boys, who began to hang around together. A 'circle of friends' was how Jasmine had described it.

Jasmine was Alice's closest friend. She was lively and outspoken, the sort of person who was never afraid to give her opinion whether it was asked for or not, unlike Alice, who was quite shy by nature. Perhaps that was why the two of them got on so well together, because they complemented each other.

When she had first come to the school, making friends hadn't been easy for Alice. She had joined a year after everyone else, when her family had moved house. She'd found the experience of arriving at a school where everyone already knew each other, and was familiar with the routines and rituals, very intimidating. Alice wasn't the kind of person who could just walk up to people she'd never met before and start talking to them. So for the first few days she had wandered about like a lost soul, too embarrassed to ask the other students where she should be or what she ought to be doing next. Then one day

Jasmine had come over to Alice and started talking to her, making jokes and telling little stories as if she'd known her since nursery. She'd taken Alice under her wing, explaining who everybody was and what all the teachers were like, making Alice laugh out loud when she pointed out their odd little habits of speech or dress.

Later, Jasmine had introduced her to Phoebe, whom Alice would probably never have become friends with otherwise, since Phoebe had a kind of aloofness about her that came from being both very pretty and alarmingly intelligent. A boffin was how a lot of people described Phoebe. Alice knew perfectly well that this wasn't a nickname to be desired. It was good to be clever, but it was best not to make it too obvious. However, when Alice got to know her better, she found that Phoebe had her problems just like everyone else, and they were mostly to do with her pushy parents.

For the next two years the three of them had been inseparable, walking about arm in arm, consoling each other when times were hard and celebrating together when they were on a winning streak. So close you couldn't have slid a sheet of paper between them. But this summer a change had come about. The fortress of their friendship had begun to let down its drawbridge and open its gates to the army camped outside. And who were those mail-clad warriors with their bright shining swords? Why, the boys, of course. Who else?

There was Adam, probably the best-looking boy in the class, though unfortunately he knew it, and Gary, who was OK but always tried to act cool and sometimes got on Alice's nerves. And then there was Matt. He was Alice's favourite. He was dark, good-looking, though not in an obvious way, and quiet. Brooding was the word that Alice used about him. And when she said it, Jasmine and Phoebe laughed out loud because it seemed to fit so perfectly.

Alice, Jasmine, Phoebe, Adam, Gary and Matt. That was the nucleus of the circle of friends that gathered in the garden of The Eagle on Friday nights. Sometimes they were joined by others, sometimes it was just the six of them. They chose The Eagle because no one asked them how old they were as long as they were dressed up and confident, and because they liked the garden with its big wooden tables and bench seats. In the centre of the garden was a big old tree that Alice loved. Its branches had twisted and gnarled over the years and the leaves, which had been green only a few weeks ago, had all turned gold and red now and were beginning to fall to the ground one by one. It occurred to Alice, as she sipped her glass of cider, that it would not be warm enough to sit outside in the evenings for much longer.

Her thoughts were interrupted by Adam. 'Is everyone definitely going on the Cornwall trip?' he asked.

'I am,' Jasmine told him.

'So am I,' Phoebe said. 'I think it sounds really good. I've been to Cornwall before and it's lovely.'

'It's the week of my birthday,' Alice complained. 'I was going to have a party.'

'You can have one when you come back,' Adam pointed out.

Alice nodded. 'I suppose so.'

'You are coming on the trip though, aren't you?' Matt asked.

There was something about the way he said it that made Alice take notice, a very faint undertone of urgency, as if her answer was really important to him. Or maybe she had just made that up. She wasn't sure. She looked at him, wondering whether or not she was just imagining things and, as she did so, a leaf detached itself from the tree in the centre of the garden and drifted gently downwards, turning in the air as it fell. Alice felt a little thrill of pleasure run through her at the sight. She opened her mouth to say, 'Yes, Matt. I'm definitely coming,' but it was Jasmine who spoke first.

'Of course she's coming,' she said. 'Everyone's going. It's going to be really good.'

Then Phoebe started talking about the place she had stayed in Cornwall and how beautiful the sea had been. The moment passed when Alice could have looked directly back at Matt and assured him that she certainly was coming, while at the same time maybe including her own hidden message somewhere underneath the words, a message that would have made it clear that if Matt was interested in her, then she was interested in him, too. Alice felt cheated by the conversation, irritated with Jasmine for replying on her behalf, but most of all annoyed with herself for hesitating just that little bit too long. The others carried on speculating about what the trip would be like but, instead of joining in, Alice slowly drank her glass of cider and sank into her own disappointment.

2

For the next couple of weeks the echoes of that night in The Eagle had remained with Alice, reverberating dully through the days, so that she woke up each morning thinking about the opportunity she had missed. Then one day Gary came into school and announced that he was holding a party and straight away she had found herself feeling optimistic again. It wasn't his birthday or anything like that. In fact, there was no real occasion to celebrate. It was just that his parents had decided to go away for the weekend and Gary was not going with them.

Anyone who knew Gary well would have realised that leaving him in charge of their house for the night was not a good idea, but Gary's parents either didn't know their son very well or they didn't care. Naturally, the moment they informed him of their decision, he began making plans to get hold of a powerful sound system and a good supply of alcohol and started drawing up a list of people he was going to invite. In fact, he needn't have bothered with the list because once the news about the party got round, pretty much everybody who'd ever heard of Gary made a note of his address. So did plenty of people who hadn't. Gary's party was an event on the Beckerton social calendar long before it happened.

Getting ready for a party is a serious business. There are clothes to be tried on: hair to be styled and make-up to be experimented with. So Alice, Jasmine and Phoebe decided to meet at Jasmine's house beforehand. Alice arrived at about eight o'clock with a bag full of clothes and Jasmine's mother opened the door. Alice liked Jasmine's mother. She was really friendly and you could see the resemblance between mother and daughter immediately. They both had the same dark hair, olive skin and wide welcoming smiles. 'Hello Alice,' she said. 'Come on in. The others are up in Jasmine's room getting ready.'

Jasmine's room was in a state of chaos. Music was playing loudly, clothes were piled up all over the place, and Jasmine was in the process of styling Phoebe's hair with straightening irons. 'Hi,' Jasmine said as soon as Alice stepped inside. 'What kept you?'

'I couldn't decide what to wear.'

'Neither can we. Never mind. Have a glass of cider. The bottle's over on the dressing table and there are some glasses somewhere.'

Alice found a glass, poured herself some cider and sat down on the bed. The mounting sense of excitement that she had felt about the party all day long, rose by several notches now that she was in the company of her friends.

'Show us what you've brought,' Jasmine said.

Alice got out the clothes she had brought along and held up each garment for the others to consider. Soon she was trying them on and swapping them for items belonging to Phoebe or Jasmine as each outfit was assessed and either given a vote of confidence or rejected. Then, when they had finally settled on what each one would wear, they began to put on make-up. Jasmine had the biggest collection of cosmetics that anyone could possibly own, dozens of colours of eye shadow and blusher, proper make-up brushes and tubes and bottles that Alice didn't even know the purpose of.

Alice tried out lots of different shades but ended up settling for the same red-brown eye shadow that she always used. 'My eyes are such a pale colour,' she complained, 'everything else just looks weird.'

'You've got really nice eyes,' Jasmine told her. 'Hasn't she, Phoebe?'

'Definitely,' Phoebe said.

'Thanks,' said Alice, embarrassed. She felt as if she had been fishing for compliments, but she hadn't. Her eyes really were an unusual shade of blue and it was something she felt self-conscious about.

It was nearly nine o'clock before they were finally happy with their appearances. 'Well, at least we won't be the first to arrive,' Alice said, taking a last look at herself in the mirror.

'Just a minute,' Jasmine said. She got out yet another little bottle from her make-up collection.

'What's that?' Alice asked.

'The finishing touch,' Jasmine said. It was glitter. She dabbed some on Alice's shoulders and admired the result. 'Perfect,' she said. Then she did the same for Phoebe and herself. 'Right, now we're ready to face the party,' she declared.

Jasmine's mum had agreed to give them a lift and when they came downstairs her face broke into a big smile. 'Well you three look lovely, I must say,' she said. 'Now, have you got your mobile phones?'

'We've got everything,' Jasmine said.

'Let's go then.'

Alice and Phoebe sat in the back seat of the car, with Jasmine in the front beside her mother, as they drove to the party.

'Remember what I said about coming home,'

Jasmine's mother said, as they turned into Gary's road. Alice and Phoebe were sleeping over at Jasmine's house. They were all going home together in a cab.

'Yes mum,' Jasmine said. 'We're getting a taxi back and we'll be home around one.'

Her mother shook her head. '*By* one,' she said, 'not around one.'

'OK,' Jasmine agreed, raising her eyebrows.

They pulled up outside Gary's house. You could hear the music as soon as you opened the car door.

'Goodness, that sounds noisy!' Jasmine's mother said. 'I pity the neighbours. Well, enjoy yourselves.'

'We will!' all three of them chorused.

They rang the bell and the door was opened by a gangly looking boy with long, greasy hair and a rather feeble attempt at a goatee beard. He was clutching a can of lager in one hand. 'Hi girls! Welcome to the party,' he said, as he stood in the doorway, leering at them.

'Where's Gary?' Jasmine asked him.

'Who's Gary?' he replied.

'Never mind,' she said, and they pushed past him. The hall was full of people they had never seen before. They peered into the front room, which was in semi-darkness and crammed with party-goers dancing to the hypnotic music that boomed out of the sound system.

'I can't see anyone I know,' Alice shouted.

'Let's try another room,' Jasmine yelled back.

They found Gary, Adam and Matt in the kitchen and went over to say hi. Gary was speaking very loudly and swearing more than he usually did. Alice guessed he'd already had quite a lot to drink. When he went to fill up his glass she asked Matt, 'Is he OK?'

Matt nodded. 'I think so. He just started drinking a bit early.' Then he said, 'Do you fancy dancing?'

'OK,' Alice agreed.

'Great idea,' Jasmine said.

Alice had thought that Matt was just talking to her but Jasmine had obviously taken it as a general invitation, and perhaps it had been. Alice couldn't be sure and Matt gave no sign one way or the other. Phoebe said she didn't fancy dancing, so Alice, Jasmine and Matt made their way to the front room and squeezed inside. It wasn't easy to dance in there because of the number of people surrounding them, but by holding their ground they gradually created a space.

Dancing was something Alice felt reasonably confident about. Either you could feel the rhythm of the music or you couldn't. That was her opinion. And she could. She knew how to empty her mind and let the sounds flood in, so that she no longer thought about what her body was doing but allowed herself to respond to the beat instead. The other two each had their own distinctive styles of dancing. Jasmine was energetic. Her face lit up with enthusiasm and she made dramatic gestures with her hands. Matt was completely different. There was something slightly dream-like about the way he moved, as if he had passed into some sort of trance and entirely forgotten where, or even who, he was.

There were no breaks in the music, one track blending seamlessly into the next and, after a while, Alice began to feel hot and sweaty. 'I'm going to get a drink,' she told the others. Neither of them showed any sign of having heard her. Nevertheless she turned and made her way out of the room.

While Alice had been dancing, even more people had arrived and now it was absolutely chock-a-block in the hallway. She fought her way to the kitchen where she had difficulty finding something to drink from. All the glasses had been taken, but she discovered a mug that nobody seemed to have claimed. To her disappointment she found that practically everything drinkable had already been consumed. There were just a lot of empty bottles on the table. In the end she came across a can with some coke sloshing about in it and decided that would have to do.

There was no sign of Phoebe or Adam, but Gary was still standing where she had left him. He was clutching a bottle of red wine in one hand, every now and then taking a swig from it. He was talking to a boy who was wearing a T-shirt with Screw You written on it. She noticed that Gary was swaying as he spoke and that he was still speaking much too loudly. She caught a snatch of what he was saying.

'There shouldn't be any laws at all,' he declared.

'That's ridiculous,' the boy in the T-shirt said.

'Why is it ridiculous?' Gary demanded.

'Because then people would be free to steal or murder or do whatever they wanted.'

Just then Gary caught sight of Alice. He leaned over and grabbed her by the arm. 'Alice, you're neutral,' he said. 'What stops you from murdering people you dislike? Is it because there's a law against it or is it just your personality?'

She shook his hand off her arm. 'I don't want to murder anyone,' she told him.

'But if you did,' he insisted.

'That's just stupid, Gary,' she said. 'You're pissed.'

The boy in the T-shirt grinned. 'See!' he said.

'I'm not pissed,' Gary replied.

'Yes you are.'

'I'm simply pointing out that those people who want to commit a crime are going to do it anyway, whether there's a law against it or not.'

'This is a stupid conversation,' Alice said. 'I'm going back into the front room.'

Gary seemed unperturbed by her refusal to back him up. He carried on putting forward his theories about human behaviour as she made her way back out into the hall, squeezing past a couple with their eyes shut and their bodies wrapped around each other, locked together in a long and passionate kiss.

She pushed her way back into the front room and, as soon as she stepped inside, she was aware of Matt and Jasmine in the middle of the other dancers. She had been about to go over and join them but now she stood still and watched instead. They were very close together, so close that Jasmine's face was right next to Matt's and her arm was resting on his shoulder. He was saying something in her ear and she was smiling and nodding. It seemed to Alice that there was a little bubble of intimacy around them that excluded everyone else. She found herself regretting her decision to leave the room to get a drink. She had only been gone a matter of minutes but, in that time, it looked as if some sort of understanding had been reached between Jasmine and Matt and she no longer felt able to impose herself between them. Instead, she turned and left the room.

Once outside in the hallway Alice was unsure what to do next. She needed someone to talk to, someone who would take her mind off what she had just seen. But she didn't want to go back into the kitchen. Talking to Gary would be no consolation. He would just come out with a load of nonsense. She wondered where Phoebe had gone and decided to go in search of her.

The party had spread upwards from the ground floor so Alice began picking her way up the stairs. People were sitting on almost every step and on the landing at the top a queue had formed outside the bathroom. As she made her way past, she saw the gangly boy with the goatee beard who had opened the front door. He grinned when he saw her. 'Hey, it's you again,' he said. 'Enjoying the party?'

Alice shook her head. 'Not really,' she said. 'It's too crowded for me.'

He seemed undeterred by her lack of

enthusiasm. 'So, why don't we go and find somewhere a bit less crowded?' he asked.

'No thanks,' she said, beginning to move away.

'You could be making a big mistake,' he told her.

'I don't think so,' Alice replied.

More music was seeping out of one of the bedrooms, so Alice headed in that direction. She opened the door and peered inside. Through a haze of smoke, she saw that the room was full of people sitting on the floor and that a joint was in the process of being passed around. A few people looked up to see who had just come in but most took no notice. Alice stood there, hesitating for a few moments. She was curious about cannabis and felt strangely envious of the people in the room. She considered sitting down with them and waiting for someone to pass the joint to her, but something prevented her. It wasn't that she thought what they were doing was so dreadful, it was just that she didn't feel entirely ready to join in. Not just yet. Another time, perhaps. She felt certain there would be another time. She stepped back out into the hall and closed the door behind her.

The other two bedrooms were locked so Alice turned and began to head back downstairs. The boy with the goatee was still standing outside the bathroom. 'Changed your mind?' he asked when he saw her.

She shook her head but, as she pushed past him, she felt a hand on her thigh. 'Get off me!' she said, indignantly.

'What's the matter?' he asked. 'Are you a lesbian or something?'

'God, you're such an idiot!' she told him.

The boy just carried on looking pleased with himself. The idea of slapping him across the face flashed through Alice's mind, but she decided against it. He wasn't worth the trouble. Instead, she carried on down the stairs but couldn't help thinking that wandering aimlessly from room to room was not what she should be doing at a party. She made up her mind to get drunk. After all, that seemed to be what everyone else was doing. She decided to make her way back to the kitchen and try again to find some alcohol.

Gary was still arguing with the boy in the Screw You T-shirt, when she reached the kitchen, and he seemed even more agitated. 'What you don't seem to understand,' he was yelling, 'is that not everybody in the world is just out for what they can get! I mean, just because all you think about is money, that doesn't mean that everybody else has the same attitude!'

The boy in the Screw You T-shirt said something

in reply. Alice couldn't hear what it was but it seemed to really annoy Gary. 'That's a load of crap,' he said and, as he spoke, he flung out his arm for emphasis. In doing so he knocked against a girl with long blonde hair who was standing near him. She spilled her drink all over herself.

'You stupid prat!' the blonde girl said.

'Sorry,' Gary said, rather hopelessly.

The blonde girl's boyfriend swore at Gary, then shoved him hard in the chest. Gary went staggering into the drinks table, sending bottles and glasses in all directions before collapsing on to the floor. For a minute or two there was chaos as everyone in the kitchen tried to back away from the scene while, at the same time, craning their necks to see what had happened. The blonde girl dabbed at her top with a tea towel while her boyfriend continued to glare at Gary. He lay sprawled on the floor looking utterly astonished, as if he had just woken up and found himself there without any explanation.

Alice pushed through the crowd and went over to him. 'You'd better get up,' she said. 'There's broken glass all over the floor.'

Gary nodded and slowly got to his feet while Alice, who seemed to be the only one capable of doing anything other than staring at the scene, got a brush and dustpan out of the cupboard under the sink and began sweeping up the broken glass. When she'd done the best she could, she stood up. The blonde girl and her boyfriend had disappeared. In fact, most people had left the kitchen by now. But Gary was still standing there, looking as if he wasn't quite sure what had happened.

'Are you all right?' Alice asked him.

'I don't feel very well,' he said.

'Oh, God!' Alice said. 'You're not going to be sick are you?'

Gary said nothing, but he had turned completely white.

Alice tried to think what would be the best thing to do. 'Maybe you should get some fresh air,' she suggested.

Gary nodded, but he could hardly walk. Alice opened the back door and steered him out into the garden. As soon as he stepped outside he threw up.

Disgusted, Alice decided to leave him to himself. She went back into the kitchen to find Jasmine and Matt waiting for her. Someone had told them that Gary had been in a fight.

'He hasn't been in a fight,' Alice assured them. 'Someone just pushed him over and now he's being sick in the garden.'

'Gross!' Jasmine said.

'The neighbours have just been round to complain about the noise,' Matt said. 'And some girl's had her bag stolen.'

The two of them were behaving perfectly normally. The bubble of intimacy that had seemed to surround them in the living room had disappeared and Alice wondered whether perhaps she had been mistaken after all.

Gary reappeared just then, looking terrible. 'Are you OK?' Matt asked him.

'I want to go to bed,' Gary said.

'You can't do that, ' Alice told him. 'Someone's got to get this party under control.'

'The party's over,' Gary said.

'But the house is still full of people,' Alice pointed out.

'I don't care,' he replied. 'The party's over!' Gary spoke more loudly this time. The other people in the kitchen looked in his direction, but no one took any notice.

In the end, it was Alice who took control. She surprised herself by that. 'Go and turn on all the lights and ask the DJ to turn off the music,' she told Gary. He did as she told him. When the thumping rhythm had stopped, she called out, 'The party's over. Can everyone go home now please?' She felt embarrassed, her voice sounding very small and ineffectual but then Jasmine and Matt joined her. They went around the room asking everyone to leave and, though people were very reluctant at first, they did begin slowly to get the message.

Now that the lights were on, you could see what a mess the house was in. There were plastic cups, beer cans and cigarette butts everywhere. Drink had been spilled on the carpet in several places. Gary groaned. 'My parents are going to go mad,' he said.

'We'll get it all cleared up,' Alice said, as reassuringly as she could.

He didn't look convinced.

Alice found some bin liners in the kitchen. She gave them to Matt and Jasmine and asked them to pick up the cups, cans and bottles. This actually had more impact on the party-goers than anything else. Once they saw people starting to clear up, they realised that the party really was over and, one by one, they made their exits. The people who had been smoking dope in the bedroom upstairs were harder to shift. They took no notice of Alice when she asked them to leave. Then Matt had the idea of telling them that the police were outside. That did the trick. The room emptied rapidly.

As Alice was going downstairs again, she saw the door of one of the locked bedrooms open. Adam and Phoebe stepped out, looking embarrassed when they saw her.

'What's happening?' Phoebe asked.

'The party's over,' Alice told her. 'We're clearing up. You can help if you like.'

It was easier now that there were more people lending a hand and soon the house began to look relatively presentable. Matt found the handbag that was supposed to have been stolen. It had been shoved behind one of the sofas. And Adam discovered somebody's mobile phone in the room where people had been smoking dope. By five to one most of the people had gone home and even though the house was still going to need a lot of tidying up in the morning, Alice, Jasmine and Phoebe couldn't stay to help any longer. Jasmine had ordered a cab and now they could hear the driver sounding his horn outside.

'Come on, then,' Jasmine said.

Alice followed Jasmine out to the front door. Phoebe lingered for a few moments to say something to Adam, then she joined them.

'You're a bit of a dark horse,' Jasmine said to

Phoebe as they clambered into the taxi. 'Isn't she, Alice?'

Alice nodded. She didn't really know what to say. She had spent the whole party thinking that something had been going on between Jasmine and Matt, but all the time it had been Phoebe and Adam who'd been busy getting off with each other. If something *had* taken place between Matt and Jasmine, it seemed that it had got no further than looks and whispers.

Phoebe looked pleased with herself. 'You have to take your chances when they're offered,' she said.

'We'll remember that,' Jasmine replied. 'Won't we, Alice?'

'Yes,' Alice said. 'We certainly will.' And even though she said it in a light-hearted way, she really meant it. This was a lesson, she told herself as the cab sped through the deserted streets. And she was determined to learn it.

3

After what had happened at Gary's house, Alice went right off the idea of holding her own party. The thought of a lot of drunken people stampeding around her house no longer seemed terribly attractive. Nor was this the only effect the evening had on her. She also found that she was more uncertain about Matt. Before the party she had been reasonably confident that he was attracted to her. But now she wasn't so sure. He still seemed keen to hang around with her and Jasmine, but which one of them was he really interested in? Alice wondered if Jasmine was thinking the same thing when, a couple of weeks after the party, she asked Alice, 'So, do you fancy Matt? I mean, really fancy him.'

'A bit,' Alice said. 'Do you?'

'A bit,' Jasmine agreed. 'I mean he is good-looking.'

'Yeah.'

'But it's hard to know what he thinks about things.

He doesn't say very much.'

'No, he doesn't.'

'Do you think he's interested in anyone in particular?'

Alice shrugged. The conversation was beginning to make her feel uncomfortable. She didn't want to hear Jasmine say that she had her sights set on Matt, but she didn't quite have the confidence to come out and say so herself. She decided to change the subject. 'Phoebe and Adam have gone very lovey-dovey. They were holding hands on the way back from school yesterday. Did you notice?'

'I don't care what they do,' Jasmine said. 'That's up to them. I just think it's a pity she seems to have completely forgotten about us. I mean, how long have we been her best friends? And suddenly she's hardly got time to talk to us.'

It was true. Phoebe seemed to be so caught up in her relationship with Adam that nothing else mattered. Twice, already, she had arranged to go shopping with Jasmine and Alice at the weekend but had phoned up at the last minute to say she couldn't make it because Adam wanted her to do something else.

Things finally came to a head the following Saturday, when the three girls were supposed to be going to the cinema together. Alice and Jasmine arrived on time but there was no sign of Phoebe. They waited in the foyer for half an hour before Jasmine finally phoned and got Phoebe's mother. She seemed surprised to hear from them.

'I'm afraid Phoebe's gone round to see Adam,' her mother said rather stiffly, sounding as if she did not entirely approve of the arrangement.

'Right, that's it,' Jasmine said, when she had put her mobile phone away. 'I'm going to tell her what I think of her next time I see her.'

Privately, Alice wondered whether this was a good idea. Jasmine could be pretty scary when she wanted to be and Alice wasn't convinced that this was the right way to approach Phoebe. But there was no point in arguing with Jasmine when she was in a mood like this. Her lips were pressed together in a hard, thin line and Alice could see that she was mentally rehearsing all the things she was going to say to Phoebe.

In fact, it wasn't Jasmine who put things plainly to Phoebe. It was Alice. She was just getting ready for bed that evening when Phoebe rang. 'I'm so sorry,' she said. 'I completely forgot we were going to the cinema. Then I remembered at about nine o'clock and I tried to ring but you must have had your mobiles switched off.'

'We were watching the film,' Alice pointed out.

'I realise that. Listen, I'm really sorry. Are you totally pissed off with me?'

'Well if you want to know the truth, Phoebe, yes I am. You can't treat us like that.'

'I know. I'm sorry. It just slipped my mind.'

'Everything slips your mind at the moment,' Alice said.

'It's just so difficult,' Phoebe replied. 'I mean, Adam keeps wanting to do things together and obviously I want to do things with him but my parents are breathing down my neck all the time and then there's you guys. It all gets so complicated.'

Her explanation only made Alice more annoyed. She was sure it wasn't easy for Phoebe, but that was no excuse for arranging to meet someone and then just forgetting all about them.

'Look, don't trouble yourself on our account,' Alice said, her voice cold and hard. 'I mean, if you want to do things with us that's fine, but if you're too busy, don't arrange to meet us, then treat us like shit and then phone up and start telling me how difficult it is for you, because I'm not interested. We waited half an hour for you tonight, standing around in the foyer like a couple of lemons and that's the third time you've let us down in three weeks.'

There was silence at the other end of the line and Alice could tell that Phoebe was shocked by what she'd heard. Well, she didn't care. Phoebe needed to be told. You couldn't go messing people about and expect them to turn around and smile sweetly at you in return.

Finally, Phoebe said, 'I didn't realise it was such a big deal.'

'Of course it's a big deal, Phoebe,' Alice said. 'We're your friends, remember. You don't just forget about your friends because you've got yourself a boyfriend.'

'I haven't forgotten about you,' Phoebe protested.

'No? Well it certainly looks like it.'

There was another long pause. Then Phoebe said, 'I think I'd better go now.' She hung up.

Immediately, Alice regretted the way she'd spoken. It wasn't like her to get angry like that. Generally, she would have described herself as quite a calm person. But there had just been something about Phoebe's tone of voice that had irritated her, as if Phoebe herself knew that her explanation was pathetic. As she was thinking this, it occurred to her that Phoebe might decide she was jealous. She hoped not because she wasn't. Was she? No, of course not. All the same, she wished she hadn't said those things now. The last thing she wanted was to look like a jealous cow. It wasn't as if she fancied Adam herself. He wasn't her type, far too pleased with himself for one thing. And it wasn't that she envied Phoebe for having a boyfriend. Well, perhaps she did, a bit. But that wasn't the point. What she'd said had been entirely true; friendship wasn't something that you could just pick up and put down when it suited you.

Alice tried to put the whole conversation out of her mind but lay awake for ages that night, going over it again and again in her mind. She was still thinking about it the next morning at breakfast when the phone rang. It was Jasmine. 'What did you say to Phoebe last night?' she demanded.

'Why, what happened?'

'She phoned me this morning and she was so apologetic. I wanted to have a go at her but I couldn't because she was being so nice. She said she hadn't realised how badly she'd treated us until she spoke to you. Now she does, apparently. She said she really values our friendship and she doesn't want to lose it and she's going to do something to make up for it.'

'Like what?' Alice asked.

'I don't know. It's supposed to be a surprise.'

'What does that mean?'

'I really don't know. She just said she's going to arrange some sort of surprise as her way of apologising but she can't tell us anything about it yet because it depends on her uncle.'

'Her uncle?'

'I know. I thought that was weird but she said she'd tell us more at school next week. In the meantime, she wants me to tell you that everything you said was completely right.'

'Wow!' Alice said. 'I thought I'd really pissed her off.'

'Apparently not. What did you say to her?'

Alice described as much of her conversation with Phoebe as she could remember.

'Well it certainly did the trick,' said Jasmine.

'I wonder what this surprise is going to be?' Alice said.

'Well, hopefully we'll find out next week.'

In fact they found out the very next day. Phoebe was waiting for them at the school gate. 'I've got us free tickets for the London Eye,' she told them.

'Oh wicked!' Alice said. Despite living in London, she'd never been on the huge wheel beside the Thames.

'My uncle works for the company that runs it,' Phoebe explained. 'He said ages ago that he could get me free tickets if I wanted, but I never took him up on it. Yesterday I phoned him up and he's promised me three tickets for next Saturday, if you're up for it.'

'I'm up for it,' Alice said. She looked at Jasmine.

To her surprise, Jasmine seemed unenthusiastic. 'Isn't it a bit touristy?' she asked.

Phoebe looked crestfallen. 'Well obviously you get a lot of tourists going on it,' she said. 'But it's supposed to be really good. On a clear day, you can see all of London. But if you don't want to go…'

'Of course we want to go,' Alice said. Jasmine must still be annoyed with Phoebe, she decided. That was carrying it a bit too far, in her opinion. Phoebe was trying and Alice was prepared to meet her halfway.

Phoebe looked pleased. 'My uncle says the best time to go is early in the morning. The queues aren't so long then.'

'I thought we were getting free tickets,' Jasmine said.

'You still have to queue, even after you've got your ticket,' Phoebe explained.

Jasmine made a face.

The bell sounded for the beginning of school then. Phoebe had to rush off to see her flute teacher, which gave Alice a chance to talk to Jasmine on her own. 'I think we should give Phoebe a break,' she said. 'She's doing her best.'

'I know that,' Jasmine said. 'It's just…the London Eye.'

'What about it?'

'Well, I don't really fancy it.'

'It'll be great,' Alice said. 'It's the world's tallest observation tower. Did you know that?'

Jasmine shook her head. She seemed to be determined not to show any enthusiasm. So Alice decided to drop the subject. If Jasmine had made up her mind to be moody there was nothing she could do about it, but she was looking forward to going on the London Eye and she was certain they were going to enjoy themselves.

The only thing that did concern Alice was the weather. All week the sky was cloudy and grey and, on Thursday, it rained for nearly the whole day. 'Looks like our trip's going to be a wash out,' Jasmine said as the three girls sat in the dining hall staring out of the window. Alice couldn't help thinking that she sounded pleased at the idea.

'It could change by the weekend,' Alice pointed

out. Phoebe looked at her gratefully.

In fact, Alice's prediction turned out to be correct. When she looked out of her bedroom window on Saturday morning, there wasn't a cloud in sight. It was the perfect day to be lifted above the rooftops of London.

They had arranged to meet at the railway station at half past nine. Alice was there at twenty past. Phoebe arrived at twenty-five past but Jasmine was ten minutes late. 'I couldn't get out of bed,' she explained. 'I'm feeling a bit funny this morning.'

'In what way, funny?' Alice asked.

'I don't know. Maybe I'm coming down with something.'

Alice suspected that Jasmine was still being grumpy but she didn't want to make any more fuss about it so she made no further comment. A few minutes later the train arrived and they all got on board.

They could see the London Eye, dominating the skyline like a gigantic bicycle wheel, even before the train pulled into Waterloo station. To Alice's surprise, it seemed to be standing completely still. 'Why isn't it moving?' she asked.

'It is,' Phoebe said. 'It just goes very slowly.'

Alice wasn't sure. It still seemed to her to be stationary. But when they got off the train and joined the stream of people on the walkway that led to the South Bank, she could see that Phoebe was right, the wheel was moving ever so slowly. Now that she was closer, she could make out the people in the individual capsules.

They had to go to the ticket office to get their complimentary tickets. Then they lined up to get on board. Even this early in the morning the queue had doubled back on itself. On all sides Alice could hear different languages being spoken and it occurred to her that people had come from all over the world to visit the city which she lived in every day and simply took for granted.

At last, they reached the front of the queue. They stood behind a turnstile waiting for the next capsule to come round and be emptied of its existing passengers, so that they could step on board.

Although the wheel had seemed to be standing still from a distance, Alice now saw that it never actually stopped at all. As the capsule drew alongside them, the barrier was lowered and they stepped on board. Others pressed in behind them, then the doors were shut and their ascent began. A recorded announcement welcomed everyone on board, telling them that they would be climbing to a height of 135 metres above London, explaining where north, south, east and west lay and pointing out the location of the emergency button should any passenger be in need of assistance.

'What sort of emergency do you think they have in mind?' Alice asked. She had meant it as a joke but when she turned to Jasmine, she saw that her friend was looking very serious.

'I don't want to think about it,' she said.

Alice smiled reassuringly. 'Don't worry,' she said. 'I'll try not to break the glass.'

The capsule was roughly oval in shape with a wooden bench down the middle and glass walls that curved inwards towards the floor and ceiling. Everyone was standing against the sides, holding on to the metal handrail that ran round the edge and peering out excitedly. Alice found a place to stand and watched as the people they had left behind on the ground grew smaller and smaller. She could see the queue still shuffling forwards, and a constant stream of new arrivals joining it all the time. On the grass beside the queue a man was juggling coloured balls and a little crowd of onlookers was standing around watching him.

Alice changed her angle to look down at the river

where the wheel cast its huge shadow across the cold, grey water. A boat full of tourists was making its way upstream, leaving a trail of white foam in its wake. Alice thought she could make out the heads of the sightseers turning to look up at them as they drew level. They're watching us watching them, she thought to herself. The idea amused her.

On the opposite bank, rows and rows of buildings stretched as far as the eye could see. Here and there, the sun gleamed on windows, picking them out like a spotlight. On Alice's left, she could clearly distinguish the Houses of Parliament and the familiar shape of Big Ben. Beside her, an American couple were trying to locate Buckingham Palace. The woman asked Alice to point it out for them but Alice didn't even know in which direction they should look.

She glanced back into the capsule, wondering where Phoebe and Jasmine had got to. She saw Phoebe pressed against the opposite window, staring back in the direction they had come that morning, but Jasmine was sitting on the bench in the middle looking down at her feet. Alice went over to her. 'What's the matter?' she asked.

Jasmine said nothing. Instead she just shook her head and carried on staring at her feet.

'Why don't you come and look out the window?' Alice asked her.

'I don't like it,' Jasmine replied. She spoke very quietly, so that Alice was not sure at first what her friend had said.

'Pardon?'

'I don't like it,' Jasmine repeated. Then she added, 'I'm scared of heights.'

'You're scared of heights?'

'Ssh!' Jasmine said, looking around the capsule to see whether anyone had overheard. Satisfied that nobody was taking any notice of them, she nodded.

'You've never mentioned that before,' Alice pointed out.

'We never went anywhere high up before.'

'We're perfectly safe in here,' Alice said.

'I know,' Jasmine said, 'but I still don't like it.' She sounded like a small child who wants to be picked up by her mother.

Phoebe came over. 'We've stopped,' she announced.

Jasmine looked up at her, panic written across her face. 'What do you mean?'

'We've stopped,' Phoebe repeated. 'It happens sometimes so that elderly or disabled passengers can get on and off down below. We'll start again in a minute. Ooh! Did you feel that? I think we wobbled.'

It was true, a barely perceptible motion had passed through the capsule, as if the whole wheel had shuddered slightly, then they were in motion again. Jasmine moaned to herself. 'What's wrong?' Phoebe asked.

Alice explained that Jasmine was scared of heights.

'Why didn't you say so before you got on?'

Jasmine shrugged. 'I didn't want to spoil things,' she said. She was almost in tears.

Alice sat down beside her. 'Don't worry Jaz,' she said, putting her arm around her. 'You're going to be fine. We're here with you.'

'Yeah,' Phoebe agreed. 'We'll look after you.' She sat down on Jasmine's other side.

We must look a bit odd, Alice thought to herself, three people sitting down in the middle of the capsule while everyone else is glued to the sides looking out at the view. But of course nobody was watching them, so it didn't matter what they looked like.

From where she sat, Alice could see the great steel cables that linked the capsule to the hub of the wheel. Briefly, she wondered what would happen if one of them were to snap. But the idea didn't frighten her because she didn't really believe it would happen. She wondered whether that was the difference between her and Jasmine. Did Jasmine actually believe something terrible was going to happen? Or was it more basic than that? Was it just a physical thing that she couldn't reason herself out of?

Their capsule continued climbing into the sky until they had reached the highest point. 'We're on top of the world now,' Phoebe said, a little tactlessly, and for a short while they could see people in the capsules below looking up at them enviously. Then they began to descend and the next capsule took their place at the apex of the wheel.

'We're on the way down now,' Alice told Jasmine.

As they drew nearer to the ground the same recorded voice that had told them they would reach a height of 135 metres above London, now invited them to stand against the rear wall of the capsule if they wanted to have their photographs taken.

Phoebe stood up. 'Come on, we must get a photo done,' she said.

'Are you coming, Jasmine?' Alice asked.

Jasmine shook her head. 'You go,' she said.

Alice hesitated. The trip had been more or less ruined but she still wanted to have something to remember it by. 'Come on, Jasmine,' she said. 'We're nearly at the bottom.'

Reluctantly, Jasmine got up and the three of them went and stood beside the other people in the capsule. 'Where's the camera?' Alice asked.

Phoebe pointed downwards to where twin cameras were mounted on the scaffolding of the wheel. 'Smile!' she said.

Alice smiled as enthusiastically as she could but Jasmine continued to look miserable. There was a flash, then they were past the cameras and heading for the disembarkation point.

'Sorry if I spoilt things,' Jasmine said, after they had stepped out of the capsule.

'Don't worry about it,' Alice told her. 'We still had fun, didn't we, Phoebe?'

'Of course.'

As they stood in the queue for their photographs, Jasmine began to cheer up visibly. She tried to make light of her experience in the capsule, holding out her hands in front of her to show Alice and Phoebe that they were still shaking.

When the woman in the kiosk showed them their photograph, Jasmine groaned and made a cross with her fingers as if she was warding off a vampire. 'I look like something from a horror movie,' she said. 'I'm not getting one of those.'

Undeterred, Alice and Phoebe each bought a print.

On the way back to the station, a thought suddenly occurred to Alice. 'What about the trip to Cornwall?' she asked Jasmine. 'We're supposed to be going rock-climbing, aren't we?'

'I'm not doing that bit,' Jasmine declared firmly.

'What if you have to?'

'They can't make me,' Jasmine said. 'I'm not doing it, no matter what anyone says.'

They didn't talk any more about Jasmine's fear of heights after that, but over the next few weeks Alice couldn't help noticing that things had changed between the three of them. Phoebe made more of an effort to be friends but it was never quite the same as it had been. She was a different person now, more distant, as if her relationship with Adam had somehow made her grow away from Alice and Jasmine and there was nothing that she could do to disguise that fact, no matter how hard she tried.

However, the opposite appeared to be true of Jasmine. She seemed to have become more in need of reassurance, as if the balance of power between her and Alice had shifted, subtly but critically, during their trip on the London Eye. For all the time that

Alice had known her, Jasmine had been the one in control, the decision-maker. Now, she was more hesitant, waiting to see what Alice thought about something before making up her mind. She's lost some of her confidence, Alice thought to herself. And it struck her, for the first time, that an individual's personality was not necessarily a fixed thing. It could change with circumstances and even a small thing, like a morning's sightseeing, could be the catalyst that brought that change about. Of course, she was still essentially the same old Jasmine. But the memory of that afternoon's events remained with her distantly, with all three of them, as the weeks went by and Cornwall drew closer.

4

There were a number of things that Alice needed to get sorted out before the trip. She had to buy a rucksack, which was easy enough, and a new coat, which was much more difficult. It had to be properly rainproof, the sort of coat that you would wear when walking by the sea in October. But Alice was also determined that it should be reasonably fashionable. And that proved quite a challenge. She went to the shopping centre with her mother one Saturday and they spent hours trekking from one store to another, trying on coats that were either the wrong colour or the wrong size or not sufficiently waterproof.

'The trouble with you is that you're too fussy,' her mother said, wearily. She had just been back to the car park to buy another parking ticket because the last one had expired. 'We're never going to get a coat at this rate.'

But Alice knew exactly what she wanted. She could see a picture of it in her head: sturdy but stylish, the kind of coat you could wear in the country but also in the city. Finding that coat was a different matter, however, and they were on the point of giving up altogether when at last she struck lucky. There it was, in the only shop they had not yet tried. It was weatherproof, fashionable and just the right size. Unfortunately it cost much more than Alice's mother had expected to spend.

Alice bit her lip and said nothing, and eventually her mother sighed and nodded her head reluctantly. 'It does suit you,' she agreed. 'I have to admit that. Just don't lose it, that's all.'

Alice grinned delightedly. 'Thanks Mum,' she said.

Afterwards they sat in a café drinking coffee and eating doughnuts. At least, Alice had a doughnut. Her mother, who was on a diet, just looked on rather enviously. 'Alice, you will behave sensibly when you go on this trip, won't you?' she asked.

'Of course I will Mum. I always behave sensibly.'

Her mother gave a wry smile. 'I'm not sure about that,' she said. 'I know what you, Jasmine and Phoebe are like when you get together.'

Alice finished her doughnut and licked her fingers. 'We don't hang around with Phoebe so much these days,' she said.

Immediately afterwards, she regretted being so open, because her mother looked concerned. 'Why not?' she asked, frowning. 'You haven't fallen out with her, have you?'

Alice shook her head. 'She's just got a boyfriend, that's all.'

'I shouldn't worry,' her mother said. 'I don't suppose it will last. She'll be wanting to hang around with you and Jasmine again before very long.'

'Why do you say that?' Alice asked.

'Well, she's only sixteen.'

'You think that isn't old enough to know her own minds?'

'I don't mean that,' her mother replied quickly.

'What do you mean then?'

'I just think that at your age people try things out, experiment a bit and that's the way it should be.'

Alice did not feel entirely satisfied with her mother's response. She was still quite sure that her mother regarded her and her friends as little children but she could see there was no point in pursuing the matter.

For a long time, the trip to Cornwall had seemed very distant. But now time itself seemed to pick up speed and the date of her departure grew closer and closer until it was difficult to think about anything else. When she woke up on the Saturday of departure, she found that it was a bright, clear morning like the one on which they had visited the London Eye. She wasted no time in getting dressed and bringing down her rucksack, which she had packed the night before. Then she opened the front door and stepped outside. It was a little windy but very mild, exactly the right sort of weather to be starting a journey.

Her mother fussed about, making her eat a big breakfast, while her father insisted on checking everything over and over again until he was completely satisfied that Alice had not forgotten anything. 'I bet I'll have twice as much luggage as everybody else,' Alice complained as she heaved her rucksack into the boot of the car.

'Better too much than too little,' her father replied.

The coach was already waiting outside the school gates when they arrived, the students who were going on the trip standing in a little group beside it.

'You will remember to be careful?' her mother said when they had parked on the opposite side of the road.

'Of course I will.'

Alice gave her mum a reassuring kiss on the cheek.

Her father took Alice's rucksack out of the boot and handed it to her. 'Have a good time,' he said hugging her.

'Thanks,' Alice said.

'And enjoy your birthday,' her mother added. 'Don't forget that there'll be lots of presents waiting for you when you get home.'

Mr Carmody was walking about with a clipboard, ticking off people's names as they arrived. Two other teachers, Ms Wilkinson and Ms Lucey, were also coming. They both taught English. Ms Wilkinson was a small grey-haired woman who'd been at the school so long that people said it had been built around her. Ms Lucey was fairly new. She was from New Zealand and had long reddish-brown hair and freckles. In her jeans and anorak, she looked more like a student than a teacher. Alice soon saw that she had been wrong about having twice as much luggage as everyone else. Some people had brought huge rucksacks. Matt had even brought his guitar.

'Can I have your attention?' Mr Carmody said, when everybody had arrived. 'In a minute, we'll be getting on board the coach and I'd just like to repeat what I've already told you. We want you to enjoy this trip, but we expect you to behave responsibly at all times. Just because we're going to be letting our hair down, that doesn't mean we have to let our standards drop as well.'

It was a typical Mr Carmody speech, well-meaning but deeply boring. 'Right then,' he concluded. 'When you've all got your rucksacks stowed in the luggage compartment, remembering to keep everything you'll need for the journey with you, I want you to find your seats in a nice, orderly fashion.'

Of course, what followed was a disorderly scramble but eventually everyone was on board. The driver started up the engine and, as the parents stood beside their cars and waved, the coach pulled away and the journey began.

It was a very long drive and though everyone started off full of high spirits, making jokes and laughing, they were soon lulled into a sleepy state, listening to music, reading magazines and playing computer games. Mr Carmody had already briefed them about the importance of bringing along something to keep them occupied and Alice had brought a book of crosswords and other puzzles, which she shared with Jasmine. But, after a while, Alice found that trying to read while the coach ploughed through the traffic made her feel distinctly queasy. Instead, she closed her eyes and tried to doze. She hadn't slept particularly well the night before and it seemed a good way to pass the time.

They stopped several times at service stations, where everyone climbed out to stretch their legs and use the facilities, before reluctantly getting back on board to resume the journey. The sky outside grew greyer as the day went on and, after a while, drops of rain began to appear on the windows. Soon they were driving through a real downpour and you could hardly see anything through the glass. Then the weather changed again and the late afternoon was lit up by autumn sunshine.

It was mid-afternoon before they drove across the Tamar Bridge and finally entered the county of Cornwall. Mr Carmody stood at the front of the coach telling them all about the history of Cornwall, how ever since the Romans, people had dug deep into the earth to mine copper, lead and tin and how the inhabitants of the county had spoken an entirely different language to the rest of England for hundreds of years.

'Are we nearly there yet?' Jasmine asked.

'We're still a couple of hours away,' Mr Carmody replied.

Everybody groaned.

But at last they arrived at the hostel, a modern building erected beside what looked like an old stone tower which, Mr Carmody informed them, was the remains of an old tin mine.

Alice could smell the sea as soon as she stepped off the coach. Even though she was weary and stiff, there was something quite exhilarating about the salty air.

Once they were inside the hostel, Mr Carmody took the boys to their dormitory, while Ms Lucey showed the girls where they would be sleeping. The dormitories were occupied by twin rows of single beds. Alice, Jasmine and Phoebe chose adjacent beds. Jasmine took the middle of the three. When they'd unpacked, they made their way to the dining room, where a hot meal was waiting for them. It wasn't exactly haute cuisine. In fact it was burgers, baked beans and oven chips followed by Arctic Roll, all washed down with orange squash from plastic beakers. But Alice was so hungry that it seemed like the best meal she had ever eaten.

'This meal was kindly prepared for us by the hostel staff,' Mr Carmody told them when they'd finished. 'But, from tomorrow morning, you'll be doing your own cooking, and you'll be clearing up after yourselves as well. We'll divide you into teams and the different teams will be given different tasks. Some of you will be making breakfast, some of you will be preparing packed lunches, some of you will be clearing up. And I expect *everyone* to pull their weight.

'Now, in a minute,' he went on, 'we're going to go down and take a look at the sea. But, before we do, I'm just going to repeat what I said earlier. We're responsible for your safety and we'll do everything we can to discharge that responsibility but you're responsible for yourselves as well. Is that clear?'

There was a general murmur of agreement.

'Good. Now go and get your coats and meet me back here in five minutes.'

The sun was already beginning to set as everyone made their way out of the hostel, following a path that led through some fields to a point of rock overlooking the sea. They stood behind a wide stone wall and looked out at the great stretch of water, the colour of beaten metal. A ribbon of gold ran away from them across the waves, a path leading to the setting sun, which hung, like a great red ball, on the horizon. As they stood there, they could hear the sound that the waves made drawing pebbles up and down the beach and from somewhere above their heads came the melancholy cry of a seabird.

They stayed until the sun sank below the horizon and Alice found herself shivering as the temperature began to drop. All the same, she felt as though she could have gazed at the water until it was completely dark. There was something awesome about the sheer size of the sea, the waves looking as though they were muscles rippling below the skin of some gigantic animal.

'The tide is in at the moment,' Mr Carmody told them, 'but tomorrow you'll be able to walk along the beach, using all your senses, awakening your creativity. I'm hoping for some very good pieces of writing because I know we've got some excellent writers among you. But, for now, I think it's time we went back to the hostel.'

It felt almost painful parting with the sea so soon. But there was consolation in the thought of the days that lay ahead.

'This is going to be a really good week,' Alice said, as she and Jasmine walked back together.

Jasmine nodded. 'I hope the weather's nice,' she said. 'A week of sea, sun and sex, that's what I'm looking forward to.'

'Sex?' Alice said. 'I didn't know that was on the agenda.'

Jasmine grinned and shrugged. 'Well, you never know,' she said. 'Some of us might get lucky.'

5

Alice was sitting cross-legged on the floor watching the way smoke hung in the air above her head. On her left a girl with long blonde hair was smoking a joint. Alice recognised her, though she couldn't remember where she'd seen her before. On her right a boy with a goatee beard was grinning at her. 'I see you changed your mind,' he said. She remembered him all right and she was irritated to find herself sitting next to him.

Alice thought about getting up but hesitated because it occurred to her that the girl with the blonde hair was bound to pass her the joint at any moment. She settled for turning her back on the boy with the goatee beard. He wasn't her biggest problem, anyway. Much more important was the fact that her mother was downstairs looking for her. She knew this because Jasmine had told her earlier, though where Jasmine was right now, she couldn't remember. Her mother might even be making her way up the stairs at this moment. Alice needed to know what her mum had said when Jasmine spoke to her, but she couldn't think where Jasmine had gone and as she looked around the room it became more and more difficult to see. The place seemed to be filling up with smoke.

Alice tried to get to her feet but found, for some reason, that she couldn't move. Then the girl with the blonde hair turned and looked at her. She held the joint towards Alice and smiled but it wasn't a nice smile. It was a smile that said she thought Alice shouldn't really be there because she was only a child. Alice was about to make a remark to show that she knew just what the blonde girl was thinking and that it didn't bother her at all when she realised someone was calling her. She had a terrible feeling it might be her mother.

'Time to wake up, everyone,' Ms Lucey was saying. 'Come on now, you've got fifteen minutes to get dressed and make your way to the dining room.' She was standing in the middle of the dormitory clapping her hands together and looking much more bright and cheerful than anybody had a right to be first thing in the morning. 'Is everyone awake?' she continued. 'Good. Now we've got a full day ahead of us, so let's not waste any time. I'll see you all in fifteen minutes.'

Alice propped herself up and turned her head to see Jasmine's sleepy face peering at her from the next bed. 'God, that was a bit of a shock,' she said.

'I didn't know where I was when I woke up,' Jasmine agreed.

'Neither did I,' Alice replied. She pulled back the duvet and swung her legs out of bed. It was colder than she'd expected.

On the other side, Phoebe yawned and sat up. 'I hope we get a good breakfast,' she said. 'I'm starving.'

'We have to make our own breakfast, remember,' Alice told her.

'Let's get moving then,' Jasmine said, 'otherwise I'm going to die of hunger.'

The three girls picked up their towels and wash bags and made their way to the bathroom. It was only while she was standing under the shower that Alice realised today was the last day she would be fifteen. Tomorrow was her birthday, though somehow it didn't seem to have quite the significance here in the hostel that it would have done at home. She wondered whether she would feel any different tomorrow.

When they were finally washed and dressed, they

found Mr Carmody waiting for them in the dining room. Like Ms Lucey, he was bright and breezy. He told them they'd been put in groups of four and read out the names of those in each group. Alice was pleased to discover that she Jasmine, Matt and Gary were all in the same group. They had been given the job of making tea and toast and setting out bowls of cornflakes. Other groups were put in charge of clearing up afterwards or making packed lunches. It turned out to be good fun. Everyone was happy because it was the first morning of the trip and the sun streaming through the windows showed that it was going to be a lovely day.

They soon established a little production line. Gary was in charge of making the toast, Alice and Jasmine did the buttering and Matt put out the cornflakes. As they worked, they chatted, though it was Jasmine who did most of the talking. She seemed especially lively that morning and, after a while, Alice couldn't help wondering whether her enthusiasm didn't have something to do with Matt being part of the group. Of course, there was nothing wrong with that. She herself had felt a little buzz of pleasure when she'd learned that Mr Carmody had put her and Matt in the same group. And it was in Jasmine's nature to be talkative. All the same, that morning Alice couldn't help feeling that some of it was calculated, as if Jasmine wanted to dominate the conversation so that she could keep the spotlight trained on herself. A couple of times she talked right over Alice when Alice was trying to say something.

Nevertheless, they managed to perform their task without any real problems, apart from the fact that Gary burnt about six slices of toast because he kept setting the toaster too high. By half past eight, the whole group was sitting down to breakfast.

'Make sure you have enough to eat,' Ms Lucey told them. 'You'll be getting plenty of exercise later.'

After they'd eaten, Ms Wilkinson handed out notebooks with stiff blue covers. 'These are your journals,' she informed them. 'You'll be using them to record your experiences during the week. So, write your name in the front and look after them. You'll need to bring them with you this morning.'

Then Mr Carmody announced that they were going to a beach that was famous for its fossils. They would be travelling in two separate minibuses. Half the group would be travelling with him and the other half with Ms Lucey and Ms Wilkinson.

Jasmine, Alice, Gary, Matt, Phoebe and Adam were all in the first minibus and, for a change, Phoebe sat with Alice and Jasmine rather than Adam.

Perhaps the thrill of being part of a couple is beginning to wear off, Alice thought to herself.

As usual, Mr Carmody kept up a running commentary as he drove, pointing out features of the landscape and describing events from the history of the area. 'I wonder if he talks all the time when he's at home?' Jasmine said.

'I feel sorry for his wife if he does,' Phoebe replied.

They all laughed at that, but good-naturedly because Mr Carmody was all right, really. They could have had someone much worse in charge of the trip.

They drove for about forty minutes before arriving at the beach. Then they clambered out of the minibus and stood gazing at the sea which was deep green, though further out the breakers were tipped with white.

'You can see why people sometimes call the waves white horses,' Jasmine said.

It was true. Alice could see exactly how the ribbons of foam looked like the manes of great horses galloping beneath the water.

'Because of an accident of geology, this beach is a particularly good site for fossils,' Mr Carmody told them. 'People come here from all over the place to look for them. So if you're lucky, you might find a souvenir to bring back with you. What we're going to do this morning is walk a little way along the beach, then find a nice sheltered spot to do some writing. You don't have to stick together in a group but nobody is to get out of sight of myself, Ms Lucey or Ms Wilkinson. Is that clear?'

There was a chorus of agreement before the students scrambled over a huddle of black rocks littered with seaweed and debris that the sea had left behind, then across a band of shingle and down to the wide expanse of grey-brown sand.

Alice scanned the pebbles in front of her as she walked. She found stones with holes in them, as though they had contained bubbles that had burst long ago; she found shiny white stones like marble and others that were marked with traces of red, green and even purple, but no fossils.

It was Gary who made the first discovery and he called out to the others to come and look. The fossil was much bigger than Alice had expected: a huge round black rock in which a white spiral had been embedded, looking almost as though someone had drawn it on with a piece of chalk. 'Shame it's too big to carry,' Gary said.

A girl called Deenie discovered a smaller fossil a few minutes later. It was nothing spectacular, just a fragment of dull grey stone that nestled in the palm of her hand. You had to look hard at it to see the pattern but it was there, a circle of white lines radiating out from the centre, like a child's drawing of the sun. Deenie was pleased with her find, especially when Mr Carmody told her that it was probably three hundred million years old.

However, it was Jasmine who came up with a real treasure. She and Alice were walking along together when suddenly Jasmine bent down and picked something up. 'Oh, wow! Look at this!' she exclaimed.

Alice looked at what her friend held. It was a flat black stone. At its heart was the petrified ghost of some ancient creature that had died millions of years earlier. 'It's beautiful!' Alice said.

Jasmine showed her find to Mr Carmody. 'Well done!' he said. 'This is a particularly good specimen. Fossils like this used to be known locally as mermaids' earrings.'

Jasmine held the stone up against her ear. 'Do you think it suits me?' she asked.

Mr Carmody laughed. 'You need to find the other one now,' he told her.

After walking along the beach for a little while longer, during which time Alice continued to pick up likely looking stones and examine them without success, Mr Carmody announced that it was time to stop and do some work. They each had to find their own spot, he said, because their writing was something he wanted them to do by themselves.

Alice settled for a rock at the base of the cliffs. Here, she was out of the wind and found it easier to think. She opened her journal and wrote the date at the top of the page. Then she considered what she should write next. Mr Carmody had told them that they could write anything they liked, which Alice didn't find particularly helpful. She wasn't even sure whether she was supposed to write a poem, a story, a description or an account of what they had done so far. She thought about asking Mr Carmody for some help but everyone else seemed to be getting on with the task. Even the teachers were sitting on rocks, writing.

She looked around her at the little piles of seaweed and driftwood that the waves had tossed up on to the rocks. Then she stared out towards the sea, hoping for inspiration. Instead she found herself remembering the dream from which Ms Lucey had so brutally woken her that morning. The sense of helplessness that she'd experienced because of the knowledge that her mother was downstairs looking for her while she was upstairs waiting for someone to pass her a joint. She also remembered the way she'd looked around the room for Jasmine, certain that her friend would be able to help. She began to write. 'Sometimes, I feel like a piece of driftwood, tossed about on the waves, not in charge of my own fate, but going wherever the currents take me.' Then she paused, uncertain how to go on. After a moment, she scribbled out what she had written and decided to begin again.

By the time Ms Lucey came round to tell them it was time to stop, Alice had managed to write two and a half pages. It was not like her first sentence. Instead it was simply an account of what they had done on the trip so far, the journey to the hostel, watching the sun set over the sea and the walk along the beach. It was boring. She knew it. And it was boring because she had opted for the easy way out. But she hadn't known what else to do. It was all very well for Mr Carmody to tell them to write about anything they liked but what if nothing came into your head? She wondered what Jasmine had written.

'A poem,' Jasmine told her, as they walked back along the beach together.

'I was going to write a poem,' Alice said, 'but then I decided not to.'

The students ate their sandwiches sitting at wooden tables in the car park. Then Mr Carmody told them they were going to visit a nearby town called Belmouth. 'It's a very picturesque little place,' he told them. 'I believe it's been used as a location in a number of films because the high street is so unspoilt. Naturally, we want it to remain that way so I expect you all to be on your best behaviour. I'm going to give you a couple of hours to wander about by yourselves and I'm sure that you won't let me down by getting up to any mischief.'

'Us? Get up to mischief?' Jasmine said, with a cheeky grin. 'We wouldn't do that, sir.'

Mr Carmody nodded. 'I'm pleased to hear it, Jasmine,' he said.

Belmouth was as pretty as Mr Carmody had promised. It was a town that seemed to be full of twists and turns, nooks and crannies. Alice, Jasmine, Phoebe, Adam, Gary and Matt wandered through the tiny streets where shops sold home-made fudge, beautiful shells and crystals or books full of stories about the sea and smugglers. Afterwards, they went down to the harbour and looked out to sea, trying to decide whether the tide was coming in or going out. 'It must be coming in,' Adam said, 'because it was out this morning.'

'How often does it come in and out?' Alice asked.

Gary said he thought it was twice, but no one was completely sure. 'We're such a bunch of land-lubbers,' Jasmine said.

That started the boys doing pirate impersonations and making feeble jokes about pieces of eight and barrels of rum. It was all very silly but very good fun. Then Gary said, 'Who fancies a quick drink before we have to go back to the minibus?'

'Have we got time?' Adam asked.

'If we get a move on,' Gary said. 'Come on. We passed a really nice little pub on the way here.'

The bar of The Fisherman's Rest was low and dark. You had to bend down to avoid hitting your head on a beam just inside the door. The place was hung with fishing nets and lobster pots and there were stuffed fish on the walls in glass cases. The landlord, a red-faced, bald-headed man, looked doubtfully at them when they first walked in, but he served them all the same. They found themselves a table in a quiet corner.

'God, what is this music,' Gary said when they had sat down. Some unrecognisable pop music from a much earlier era was blasting from speakers on either side of them.

'I reckon it's from the landlord's own collection,' Matt said.

'It is pretty dire,' Adam agreed. 'But it sort of goes with the place, don't you think?'

They began to talk about music then and soon the boys were deep in a discussion of groups that they liked. They seemed to be vying with each other to come up with ever more obscure names. Alice had more or less stopped listening and was thinking instead about the beach they had been walking along that morning when Gary suddenly turned to her and said, 'So what do you think of the album, Alice?'

'What album?'

He mentioned a name that meant nothing at all to her. 'I don't know. I haven't heard it,' she told him.

'You haven't heard it!' Gary shook his head sadly. 'Not girly enough for you, I expect.' Before Alice could reply he had turned to Jasmine. 'I suppose you haven't heard it either?' he said.

'Yes I have as a matter of fact,' Jasmine said. 'I really like it.'

Alice felt like throwing something at Gary but she said nothing. If he wanted to act like an expert on everything, that was up to him. But she couldn't help wondering whether Jasmine had really listened to the obscure album or whether she was pretending for the sake of appearances.

'Just think,' Adam said, changing the subject. 'Everyone else is back at school sitting through lessons right now and here we are in the pub having a drink.'

'It's all part of our education,' Jasmine pointed out.

'I just hope Mr Carmody doesn't come in here,' Phoebe said.

'Carmody's all right,' Matt declared. 'He probably knew we'd end up in the pub. Just as long as we don't cause any trouble, he doesn't care what we get up to.'

'I think there's something going on between him and Ms Lucey,' Gary said.

'Don't be ridiculous,' Alice told him. 'He's old enough to be her father.' She wasn't going to let him get away with that. She was still irritated with him over his comments a moment ago. Besides, she liked Mr Carmody and Ms Lucey and she didn't think it was fair to start gossiping about them.

'Maybe she goes for older men,' Gary suggested. 'Some women do.'

'Listen to the expert speaking,' Alice said.

Gary made a bow. 'I'm glad you recognise one when you see one.'

'What evidence have you got, anyway?' Phoebe

asked him.

'Well, I haven't exactly got any evidence,' Gary said. 'It's just a feeling, you know. A hunch. I reckon they're just waiting for a chance to give Ms Wilkinson the slip and nip behind the bushes.'

'You've got a warped mind Gary,' Alice told him.

Gary shook his head. 'You just don't understand the male psyche, Alice. Maybe when you grow up you'll look at things differently.'

'Oh shut up!' Alice said.

'Take no notice of him,' Jasmine told her. 'He's just trying to be clever.'

'I don't have to try,' Gary said. 'It comes naturally.'

Alice would have liked to come out with some really cutting comment but before she could do so, Phoebe looked at her watch. 'Hey, we haven't got much time left,' she said. 'We're supposed to be back at the minibus by four o'clock and it's five to now.'

Everyone hurriedly finished their drinks. Then they got up and made their way out of the pub. As they stepped outside, Alice found herself standing beside Matt. 'You don't want to take any notice of Gary,' he said.

'I don't,' Alice replied.

'He doesn't mean any harm. He just tries too hard sometimes.'

'Yeah, I suppose so.'

Jasmine appeared beside them then, followed by Phoebe, Adam and Gary, so there was no chance to continue their conversation. Instead, they all walked back to the car park together.

Alice still felt annoyed with Gary and with herself for not coming up with an answer quickly enough, but she also felt grateful to Matt for his thoughtful words. He didn't have a lot to say for himself, like Gary, but he wasn't shy either. He only spoke when he had something worth saying and that was a quality Alice admired. She watched him walking a few paces ahead of her, listening to something Adam was saying, reaching up with his hand to brush back the hair that flopped over his forehead, and she smiled to herself.

'What are you smiling about?' Jasmine asked her.

'Oh, nothing,' Alice said, but she wondered whether this would be the week that she found out something about the male psyche.

6

That evening it was the turn of a different group of students to take care of the catering so those who weren't involved were allowed free time. Some of them hung around the hostel's recreation room, which boasted two pool tables and a television, but Alice and Jasmine decided to go for a walk and examine the remains of the old mine nearby.

The building was no more than a shell built out of large, uneven blocks of stone, with grass growing up through the floor and holes where the windows and doors had been, like gaps in a row of teeth. Mr Carmody had told them earlier that this was where the miners had come to collect their wages at the end of each week. Alice imagined a long line of men in old-fashioned clothes, their faces blackened from their work, each waiting patiently to be handed a little pile of coins.

'I wonder what it was like working underground all day long?' Jasmine said when they were standing inside the building.

'I expect they got used to it,' Alice replied, looking up through the roof at the little patch of sky above them.

Jasmine shook her head. 'I would never have got used to it. Imagine all those tons of earth and rock, just waiting to collapse and crush you.'

'Don't!' Alice said. She heaved herself up on to one of the window ledges and sat there, swinging her legs.

Jasmine sat on the ledge opposite and the two girls faced each other like pieces across a chess board. 'Do you ever wish you were different?' Jasmine asked.

'In what way?' Alice replied.

'Just that. Do you ever wish you were a different kind of person?'

'I don't know,' Alice said. 'Sometimes, maybe. Do you?'

'I wish I was braver,' Jasmine admitted.

'But you're really brave,' Alice told her. 'You can talk to people you hardly know and you're really confident when people ask you your opinion and stuff like that.'

Jasmine shook her head. 'I wasn't very brave when we went on the London Eye,' she pointed out.

'That's vertigo,' Alice told her. 'You can't help that.'

Jasmine sighed. 'Other people don't have a problem with high places,' she said miserably. 'It didn't bother you and Phoebe, did it?'

'That doesn't mean we're braver than you, though,' Alice insisted. 'It just doesn't affect us like it affects you.'

Jasmine nodded. 'Sorry,' she said. 'I know I'm being moany.'

'Yes you are,' Alice told her with a smile. 'And this is the eve of my birthday. So it's got to stop.'

'So it is,' Jasmine said. 'Hey, do you realise that from tomorrow you'll be legally old enough to have sex?' She grinned at Alice who smiled wryly back.

'All I need is someone to have it with,' she said.

'There's always Gary,' Jasmine suggested, teasingly.

'Gary!'

'Yeah. I reckon he fancies you.'

'He thinks I need to grow up, remember?'

'He just says things like that so you'll notice him.'

'Well, he's succeeded. I have noticed him and I think he's an idiot.'

'You're not interested then?' Jasmine asked.

'Of course I'm not interested. I can't believe you're even asking me. Anyway, I think you're wrong. He doesn't fancy me. He's too busy fancying himself.' She jumped down from the window ledge. 'Come on let's go back inside. It's getting cold.'

Jasmine didn't pursue the subject any further but Alice found herself wondering about what she'd said as they queued up to get their dinner. It was burgers again with mashed potatoes and peas, followed by individual fruit pies. She and Jasmine took their trays over to one of the tables and sat down, but they'd only been there for a few minutes when they were joined by Gary himself. He sat down directly opposite Alice.

'I can't believe we've got burgers again,' he said.

'Well, at least they're not burnt like the toast,' she pointed out.

He grinned. 'One up to you,' he said.

Jasmine turned her head and gave Alice a meaningful glance but Alice ignored it. She was sure that Jasmine's suggestion wasn't true so, as she began to eat, she found herself wondering about Jasmine's reasons for making it. Was she perhaps trying to get Alice out of the way, so that she could have Matt all to herself? After all, Alice hadn't actually made it clear that she was keen on Matt, even though Jasmine had given her the chance. The trouble was, Alice didn't know what Matt thought. She wasn't even sure that *Matt* knew what he thought. She wished he would just give her some sort of clear signal.

After the dinner plates had been cleared away and stacked in the dishwasher, Mr Carmody asked them to get their journals and come back to the dining room. 'I'm going to ask you to read your work aloud,' he told them.

'I don't want to do it,' Alice said as she and Jasmine went to the dormitory to get their journals.

'Maybe you won't have to,' Jasmine suggested. 'Maybe it will just be voluntary.'

But it wasn't. Mr Carmody made them all sit in a circle. Then he announced that he was going to go round the circle asking each person in turn to read. 'I want the rest of you to listen carefully,' he said. 'Then I'd like you to give your honest reactions. But I must stress that we're looking for constructive criticism here. I don't want to hear: *I like it* or *I don't like it.* That's not good enough. I want suggestions for ways in which people can improve their writing and examples of things they've done well.'

Deenie went first. She read out a story about a little girl whose father worked in a tin mine. There had been a cave-in deep underground in one of the tunnels and she was waiting to hear whether or not he would be rescued. Finally, right at the end, she found that he was safe. It wasn't a bad story. Some people said that they would have preferred it if her father hadn't been saved but on the whole everyone liked it.

Then it was Adam's turn. He'd written a description of windsurfing along the beach, which was something he'd done in the summer. It was OK, but it didn't really have much to do with their trip to Cornwall.

After Adam, it was Alice. She'd been dreading this. She hated being the centre of attention and could feel herself going red as she began to read. She tried to get through it as quickly as she could, but Mr Carmody made her slow down and read carefully. Afterwards, she couldn't bear to look up and face the others.

But they could have been worse. A boy called James, who was always a bit of a smart alec, said it could have been more imaginative and Mr Carmody suggested that adding more description would have helped. But even though no one had really torn it to pieces, Alice knew that it was just plain boring. And what made it worse was the feeling that she could have come up with something better if only she'd been a bit more adventurous, instead of opting for the easy way out.

Eventually, it was time to move on to the next person and Alice breathed a sigh of relief as Gary began to read a story about aliens landing in Cornwall.

He'd tried to be funny, but it hadn't worked and he just ended up sounding stupid.

Out of the others, only two pieces really stood out. Matt read a description of the beach they had walked along that morning and, somehow, even though he didn't use lots of fancy words, he managed to summon up such a vivid picture of the place that Alice could close her eyes and see it stretching before her. You could tell that Mr Carmody thought it was good. He praised the way that Matt had picked out details to make the scene come to life.

The other piece of writing that really made an impact was Jasmine's. She looked apologetic when Mr Carmody turned to her. 'I've only written a short poem,' she said.

'Let's hear it, anyway,' Mr Carmody told her.

So Jasmine took a deep breath and began to read:

*'I want to pull back the grey blanket of the sea
and find the hidden world beneath
where mermaids sing sad songs of
sailors lost at sea,
drifting down through the icy water,
mouths wide open,
calling for help without ever once
disturbing the silence.'*

*

Everyone was quiet when she'd finished. Then Mr Carmody said, 'I thought that was really rather special, Jasmine.'

'Thank you, sir,' she said. 'It was the fossil that started me off.'

Mr Carmody went on to talk about her use of imagery and Alice couldn't help feeling just a tiny bit jealous. She would have liked to have heard Mr Carmody say that her piece of writing was special but she knew that it hadn't been. Afterwards, when the reading session was over, she saw Matt go over to Jasmine and she overheard him telling her how much he liked her poem. She'd been going to do exactly the same thing herself but now she stood back and watched them in just the same way she'd done at Gary's party. She found herself thinking that they looked right together, like a proper couple, and it was a thought that caused her pain.

Alice felt as if she needed to get away from everyone else, so she went outside. It had turned cold. At first, she was tempted to turn round again and go back into the warmth, but the sky stopped her. It was pitch black and studded with stars, so many more stars than she had ever seen back in Beckerton. She stared up at them and realised that she didn't know the names of any of the constellations. Was that the Plough overhead? She couldn't be sure. Then, as she watched, she saw a shooting star. It was only there for a second, but it was long enough for her to be certain she'd seen it. She'd never seen a shooting star before and to see her first one on the eve of her birthday had to be especially significant. Make a wish, she told herself. Immediately she found herself wishing that Matt would be interested in her, not Jasmine. Maybe it was mean to wish for something like that, she thought to herself afterwards, but it was what she really wanted.

7

The next morning they were woken once again by Ms Lucey. This time, Alice knew where she was as soon as she opened her eyes, but it took her a few moments to remember that it was her birthday. I should feel different, she told herself, recalling her conversation the previous evening with Jasmine, but she felt just like she always did in the mornings, slow-witted and hungry.

When Ms Lucey had gone, Jasmine got out of bed, took something out of the bedside cupboard and handed it to Alice. 'Happy birthday!' she said. There was a card and a present wrapped in layers of blue tissue paper. 'It's not your proper present,' Jasmine told her. 'That's at home. This is just for now.'

'Thank you,' Alice said, sitting up and taking them from her.

'Well, aren't you going to open them?' Jasmine asked.

'Sorry,' Alice said. 'I'm still half-asleep.' She tore

open the envelope and took out the card. On the front was a cartoon of two girls sitting back to back. Inside Jasmine had written: Happy Birthday to my best friend.

'It's lovely,' Alice said. 'Where did you get it?'

'In the Cedars,' Jasmine told her. The Cedars was the shopping mall in Beckerton where they had spent many a Saturday hanging out together.

Alice began tearing away the layers of tissue paper surrounding the present.

'I couldn't get proper wrapping paper,' Jasmine told her. 'Mr Carmody gave me this.'

Alice had been wondering what it could be. Something small and hard, that much was clear. Now, as the paper came away, she saw that it was the fossil Jasmine had found on the beach the previous morning. 'Oh no!' she said. 'I can't take this.'

'Why not?'

'Because it's yours. You found it.'

'I want you to have it.'

'Thank you,' Alice said. She was overwhelmed by Jasmine's generosity and at the same time couldn't help feeling just a little bit ashamed of herself. She had wanted to be the one who discovered a fossil to make everyone gasp and she'd been jealous of Jasmine finding one. Now Jasmine was handing it over to her, smiling and telling her it was a birthday present. She put her arms around Jasmine and hugged her. 'Thanks,' she said. 'You're a really good friend.'

Then Phoebe appeared with a card. It wasn't as nice as Jasmine's, but it was lovely to receive it, all the same. There was a picture of a bottle of champagne on the front and inside Phoebe had written: Congratulations. No one can stop you now. Alice looked at Phoebe's and Jasmine's smiling faces and it was just like old times.

'We'd better hurry up and get dressed,' Jasmine said. 'You don't want to be late for breakfast on your birthday.'

'Yeah,' Phoebe said. 'You might miss your ration of burnt toast.'

For some reason, that made Alice think about home and she began to feel nostalgic, almost weepy. If she'd been at home today, her mother would have brought her breakfast on a tray. There would have been a little pile of presents at the foot of the bed and she would have opened them one by one with cries of pleasure as each one revealed its secret. But she consoled herself with the thought that it would all be waiting for her when she got back. In the meantime Jasmine was right: there was breakfast to be eaten, burnt or not.

She wasn't prepared for what happened when she walked into the dining room a few minutes later. The moment he saw her, Mr Carmody clapped his hands and the buzz of conversation that had filled the room died away. 'OK, everybody,' he said. 'One two three...' and they all burst into a chorus of *Happy Birthday To You*. It was embarrassing, but nice as well.

After breakfast, Mr Carmody told them that they were going to walk along the coastal path. 'I'm sure I don't need to stress the importance of behaving sensibly,' he said. 'This exercise is all about observation, about using your senses to become aware of what is around you. But that doesn't mean taking any risks. So keep well away from the edge at all times and, of course, no running or pushing or fighting or any other silly behaviour.'

They began by walking down to the point of rock where they had watched the sun on their first evening. Then they set out along the path that led over the tops of the cliffs. The ground was covered with short, wiry grass. Here and there, pink flowers grew, which Mr Carmody told them were called Thrift. Far out at sea, gulls rode on the air currents, uttering their sorrowful calls. Below them, the sea seemed to boil and rage round the black and purple rocks that littered the base of the cliffs like the ruins of some gigantic building. Alice noticed that Jasmine kept well away from the edge.

'Imagine falling down there,' Gary said, coming up behind them. He always seemed to be turning up beside Alice now. Wherever she looked, there he was, coming up with some feeble joke or silly remark.

'I'd rather not imagine it,' Alice told him.

He didn't seem deterred by her lack of interest. Instead he tagged along, talking about nothing in particular. A little way ahead of them she could see Matt walking by himself looking, as he often did, completely absorbed in his thoughts.

Afterwards, they went back to the hostel for lunch and then Mr Carmody announced that they were going rock-climbing. Alice glanced at Jasmine and saw her friend's face fall. 'Are you going to speak to him?' Alice asked.

Jasmine nodded. She waited until Mr Carmody had finished making his announcements, then she went over and spoke to him quietly. Alice could see Mr Carmody nodding his head and saying something in reply but Jasmine's face didn't seem to brighten up.

'Did you tell him you don't want to do it?' Alice asked when Jasmine returned.

Jasmine nodded. She still looked unhappy.

'He told me to wait and see how I feel when we get there. He said I might change my mind when I see everybody else doing it.'

'Maybe you will,' Alice suggested.

'I don't think so,' Jasmine said. 'It sounds like my idea of hell.'

But everyone else was excited about the idea. In the minibus on the way there, Gary kept coming up with jokes about climbers and climbing and, even though they were really rather feeble, most people laughed because they were in a good mood and looking forward to the experience. Not Jasmine, though. As the journey went on she became less and less talkative, withdrawing into her own anxiety, even though Alice tried to distract her.

It was Matt who was the most enthusiastic, which was a little surprising because he was normally so quiet. But his eyes were sparkling when he said, 'I've always wanted to go climbing, ever since I saw a programme about this guy who set out to climb the seven highest peaks in the world.'

Gary interrupted him. 'Listen to this one,' he said. 'What were the climber's last words?'

'I don't know, Gary. What were the climbers last words?' Matt replied.

Gary looked delighted with himself. 'Did someone say 'ave lunch?' he declared.

The others looked at him blankly.

''Ave lunch. Avalanche,' he explained.

'Oh, God,' Matt said, 'that was terrible.'

'Please yourself,' Gary replied.

'You know what I read on the web?' Adam said. He and Phoebe had gone back to sitting together, holding hands. 'Responsible climbers are supposed to bring back their own waste with them when they come down from the mountains.'

'You mean like litter and stuff?' Alice asked.

Adam shook his head. 'I mean their own personal waste,' he said.

'Oh Adam! That is so gross!' Phoebe told him.

Adam shrugged. 'They don't have any toilets up there,' he said.

'Listen you lot,' Mr Carmody interrupted from the front of the minibus. 'We'll be arriving at the climbing centre shortly. You'll be having an introductory talk first and I want everybody to pay total attention to what the instructors tell you. No fooling about. Climbing is a very serious business. Is that clear?'

'Yes, Mr Carmody,' they all chorused back.

The climbing centre turned out to be little more

than a rather dilapidated wooden hut with peeling paint on the outside. They were shown into a dusty room and given a talk by an instructor named Ian. He was tall and thin, in his twenties, with curly black hair, dark stubble around his cheeks and a body that looked as if it was made out of knotted rope. He spoke with a strong Scottish accent and Alice wondered what could have brought him so far from his home.

Ian spent a lot of time talking about safety and the importance of following instructions. Then he showed them the equipment they would be using and explained how it worked. They each had to try on a climbing harness and he described how these were attached to the ropes, the process by which rope was gradually let out to the climber, which he called belaying, and how the same process could be used in reverse to go back down the rockface. At the end of the talk they were given boots, helmets and harnesses and they set off to walk to the cliffs, accompanied by Ian and another instructor called Dave. Like Ian, he looked well used to the outdoor life, but he was much less talkative, answering questions with no more than a nod or a shake of the head.

They walked along beside the coast for about twenty minutes before taking a path that led down to a cove. Here the cliffs sloped away from the sea in a series of massive shelf-like formations. The rocks were stark and bare of vegetation except for traces of lichen. They looked as though they were part of the landscape of some other, much less forgiving, planet.

Ian and Dave stopped beside a slab of rock that loomed about forty metres above them and thrust out towards the sea in a great triangular block. Alice thought it looked remarkably like an enormous slice of cake. 'Welcome to the Wedge,' Ian announced.

They looked at it in disbelief. 'How are we supposed to climb that?' Phoebe asked.

'Exactly as I've told you,' Ian said. 'Dave will go up first to belay you and I'll be at the bottom watching every move you make. If you find you get stuck, remain calm and listen for my instructions. But there shouldn't be any problems. It's much easier than it looks. There are plenty of hand and footholds and, when you get to the top, there's a path that leads back down to the beach again. It's well marked, but I want you to wait for the next person, then return to the beach in twos. OK?'

They all nodded. Then Dave took the rope and swarmed up to the top of the rock quite effortlessly. He let down the rope to Ian who grabbed it and turned to face them. 'Right, whose going to be first?' he asked.

Matt stepped forwards. 'I will,' he said.

Ian checked that Matt's harness was properly secured, attached the rope and explained again how the process of belaying worked. Then, when he was quite certain that Matt was ready, he showed him where to put his hands and feet to begin the climb and called out to alert Dave that they were starting.

Alice found herself biting her lip as she watched, but Matt seemed to have no difficulty. He went up the rock slowly but steadily and, when he reached the top, he scrambled over the edge and punched the air with delight.

Gary was next. He was less confident than Matt and seemed to get stuck halfway up, as if he couldn't find a handhold, but Ian called out to him, telling him exactly where to put his hands and feet and soon he was climbing again. When he had got to the top, he disappeared along the path with Matt, and the two of them reappeared a little while later looking thoroughly pleased with themselves.

One by one, other students made the climb while Alice and Jasmine stood near the back of the group, watching them. 'What are you going to do?' Alice asked, as their turn drew nearer.

'I don't know,' Jasmine replied. She was biting her fingernails.

'I thought you definitely weren't going through with it.'

'I don't want to bottle out in front of everybody, though.'

'Why don't you give it a try? You'll be all right. They won't let anything happen to us. They know what they're doing.'

Jasmine continued to gnaw at her fingernails. By now there was only a handful of students left who had not made the climb. Apart from Alice and Jasmine, Phoebe, Adam and Deenie were still waiting.

'Look, I'll go first,' Alice said. 'Then you come right after me.' But although she tried to sound encouraging, she was feeling anxious herself. Her stomach was churning as she allowed Ian to secure the rope to her harness.

But it turned out to be less difficult than she had expected. Just as Ian had told her, the cliff face offered plenty of hand and foot holds and, as long as she concentrated on what she was doing and did not think about the fact that she was getting further and further from the ground all the time, she found it was possible to climb. She did not pause, as some of the others had done. Instead she moved deliberately up the cliff, wanting to get it all over as quickly as possible until, with a huge sense of relief, she found that she had reached the top and Dave was smiling at her. 'Well done,' he said. Her legs were like jelly and they almost gave way beneath her completely when she stood up on the top of the Wedge, but she felt very proud of herself.

She wondered how Jasmine would make out and waited anxiously, hoping that her friend would be able to overcome her fear. But it was Phoebe whose face was the next to appear, looking wide-eyed and delighted to have reached the top.

'What happened to Jasmine?' Alice asked, when Phoebe had unhooked the rope from her harness.

'She says she's coming later,' Phoebe told her.

Dave pointed out the way back and they followed the path that led along the cliff and down in a wide arc to a point further along the beach. They compared notes on the way. Phoebe had really enjoyed herself. She said she wouldn't mind doing it again some time. Alice wasn't so sure. She was glad she'd made it to the top but she was in no hurry to repeat the experience.

When they got back to the others, Alice went over to talk to Jasmine.

'I can't do it,' Jasmine told her.

'It's easier than it looks,' Alice said, 'honestly. You'll be fine once you get going.'

But Jasmine wasn't really listening. She was staring straight ahead of her and it was clear that all she could hear were voices inside her head telling her she wouldn't be able to do it. Finally, when every other student had made the climb, Ian beckoned her forwards.

Jasmine stayed exactly where she was. 'I don't want to do it,' she told him.

Mr Carmody went over to her. 'It's entirely up to you, Jasmine,' he said, speaking as gently as he could. 'No one is going to make you do it, if you don't want to, but it's an opportunity that might not come your way again. If you go back without making the climb, you might regret it later.'

Jasmine shook her head. 'I don't care,' she said. 'I can't do it.' Alice could see that she was near to tears.

'OK, that's fine, Jasmine,' Mr Carmody said. 'You're perfectly entitled to make that choice.'

On the way back to the climbing centre, Jasmine didn't say a word and Alice walked along beside her in silence. She felt sorry for her friend but she couldn't help feeling that Jasmine ought to make an effort to cheer up. After all, it had been her choice not to climb the rock. No one had made her do anything against her will.

Much later, when she was back in Beckerton and the trip was only a memory, Alice wished she'd been more sympathetic. But the climb had left her feeling exhilarated and, in the minibus on the way back to the hostel, she found herself joining in with the general banter, groaning at Gary's jokes and leaving Jasmine to shake off the blues by herself.

But Jasmine was not the sort of person to stay gloomy for very long and, by the time they'd got back to the hostel and had a shower, she was beginning to return to her old lively self again. After dinner, when they were wondering what to do with the rest of the evening, she remembered that Matt had brought his guitar and she persuaded him to play something for them.

'What's he like?' Alice asked, after Matt had gone to get his guitar. 'I've never heard him play.'

Jasmine shrugged. 'Neither have I, but Adam says he's good. Anyway, we'll soon find out. Here he comes now.'

Matt came back into the dining room, carrying his guitar and looking self-conscious. He sat down on a table facing the others and began tuning up. Alice felt sorry for him. It wasn't fair to ask him to perform in front of everybody like this. She certainly wouldn't have enjoyed it. But he seemed happy enough and when he had satisfied himself that the guitar was in tune, he began to play.

She was surprised by how good he was. He didn't just strum chords. He wove in clever little lines of melody at the same time. The tune was familiar, though she wasn't sure what it was at first. The surprise came when he started to sing. His voice was strong and confident, without a hint of the nerves that he had shown earlier. And now she recognised the song. It was a chart hit, by some boy band, that she had despised when it was released because it had been so glossy and mass-produced. But Matt's version wasn't a bit like that. He'd rescued the song, given the words back their meaning and fitted a new rhythm to the tune. He looked straight ahead of him as he sang, completely absorbed in what he was doing, swaying back and forth in time to the rhythm as though the music was in control of him rather than the other way around. When he had finished, everyone in the room burst into a spontaneous round of applause and he looked around, like someone who has just woken up from a deep sleep.

'Play something else,' Alice begged him and the

others immediately joined in with her request so that Matt was soon persuaded.

He played two more well-known songs but each one had been changed so that it was almost unrecognisable at first. Halfway through the second song, Alice's mobile phone started to ring and she hurried out of the room.

It was her mother. 'Happy birthday, Alice!' she said.

'Thanks, Mum.'

'Sorry it's so late. I wanted to wait until your dad came home.'

'That's OK.'

'Are you having a nice time?'

'Yeah, really nice.' She told her mum about the cards she'd received from Jasmine and Phoebe, about Jasmine's present and about going rock-climbing. Then her father came on the line to wish her happy birthday as well. It felt strange talking to her parents like this, as if she were in a different country altogether and that they were part of a life she'd left behind. She knew it was absurd to think like that because it had only been two days since she'd last seen them, but that was how she felt.

'Well, enjoy the rest of your trip,' her mother said when her father had handed the phone back. 'We're looking forward to seeing you soon.'

'Thanks, Mum. Love you.'

When she went back to the dining room, Matt had finished singing and could not be persuaded to perform any longer. 'I've run out of songs,' he said. Then he disappeared back in the direction of the boys' dormitory clutching his guitar. The little group of students who had been his audience began to disperse as well.

'What did you think of Matt's singing?' Jasmine asked her, as they made their way to the recreation room to watch television.

'I thought he was really good,' Alice said.

'So did I,' Jasmine agreed. 'I told him he ought to go on that programme on the TV. You know, where they make you into a pop star.'

Alice felt a little stab of regret that she hadn't had the chance to tell Matt how much she'd enjoyed listening to him. It was another missed opportunity. She sighed. That seemed to be the way of things between her and Matt.

That night, after they'd all gone to bed, Alice lay in the dark with her eyes wide open, listening to the breathing of the girls in the other beds and thinking over everything that had happened since Ms Lucey had woken them that morning. It had not been the sort of birthday she'd imagined for herself when she'd been planning to hold a party and invite all her friends. There had been the cards from Phoebe and Jasmine of course, and Jasmine's unexpected present. Then the chorus of *Happy Birthday* at breakfast. But the rock-climbing had overshadowed everything. It almost seemed more important than reaching her sixteenth year and it was certainly an achievement she would always remember.

The more she thought about it, the more she was convinced that although this day was her official transition from childhood to adulthood, it was the trip itself that was the real milestone. That was what she would look back on in years to come. And it was not over yet. She had a feeling that something else had yet to take place, something that would mark the passage between the life she had lived up until now and the one that was waiting for her in the future. She could not explain where this feeling came from. It was some instinct or intuition that was beyond words. But she was convinced that whatever this thing might be, it would happen during her stay here in Cornwall. In fact, as she lay there cocooned in the darkness, she could almost feel it hovering above her in the night, like some great bird, choosing its moment to descend. She felt both excited and intimidated by the thought and she whispered into the darkness, 'Here I am. I'm waiting.' Then, deep inside herself, she felt as though something was answering. Satisfied at last, she closed her eyes and surrendered to sleep.

8

As soon as Alice woke up the next morning, she sensed that something was different. Ms Lucey was standing in the middle of the dormitory making her familiar speech, girls were sitting up in bed, rubbing the sleep from their eyes just as they had the previous morning. Nevertheless, there was a feeling in the air that had not been present before now. It wasn't long before she discovered the cause.

'It's raining,' someone said.

Alice went to the window and looked out. Sure enough, a fine mist of rain covered the landscape, blurring the edges of everything, so that the sea, which was normally visible from the dormitory window, was now just a foggy haze.

'Maybe it will clear up later,' Jasmine said.

'Let's hope so,' Alice agreed.

But by the time the girls had got dressed and made their way to the dining room, the drizzle had turned into a steady downpour. Mr Carmody, however, refused to be daunted. After breakfast, he announced that they were going to visit a nearby beach.'This isn't a holiday,' he said, when they complained about the rain. 'You're here to find inspiration for your writing, not to get a suntan.'

So, rather unenthusiastically, they all climbed into the minibuses and drove to the beach. The jokes and laughter that had accompanied the previous day's trip to the climbing centre were noticeably absent and the atmosphere was subdued. The weather seemed to be worsening with every mile and, by the time they arrived at the beach, the wind was blowing strongly. As they climbed out of the minibus, the rain drove into their faces like handfuls of needles.

'This is horrible,' Alice said.

They made their way on to the beach and stood looking out at the foam-flecked waves. A grey sky was draped over a slate-coloured sea so that it was hard to tell where the water ended and the clouds began. Now that they were here, it was not clear what Mr Carmody planned to do next. Walking along the strand was obviously out of the question as the wind was already whipping up spray and, further along the cove where rocks jutted out into the water, the waves were beginning to look a little dangerous. So they remained where they were, staring out at the uncompromising demonstration of the strength of nature.

It was bitterly cold and the damp seemed to penetrate right through to Alice's bones. Nevertheless, she did not want to leave. There was something compelling about the sea when it was like this, like the sight of some enormous beast slowly but steadily beginning to rouse itself.

Finally, Mr Carmody must have decided that it was not wise to remain there any longer. 'All right,' he said, 'I think perhaps we've seen enough.'

'What was the point of that then, sir?' Gary asked when they were back in the shelter of the minibus.

'The point of it,' Mr Carmody said, in a rather strained voice, 'is that we're here to experience what Cornwall has to offer us – both good and bad.'

'We've experienced it now. Can we go home?' Gary continued.

'That's exactly what we're doing,' Mr Carmody pointed out, stiffly.

When they finally got back to the hostel, the first thing they had to do was get dry again. The boys and girls went to their separate dormitories and Ms Wilkinson went round to see all the girls, checking that everyone was OK and tut-tutting about the state they were in. 'I don't think she approved of our wet-weather excursion,' Alice said, when the teacher was out of earshot.

'Well, I agree with her,' Jasmine said. 'Mr Carmody must be bonkers, making us go out in that.'

When everyone had got changed and hung their wet clothes over the radiators to dry, they made their way back to the dining room, where Mr Carmody told them they were to spend the rest of the morning writing in their journals. Alice sighed. Writing was the one thing about the trip she did not enjoy. Nevertheless, she sat down at a table, opened her journal and stared at the blank page, waiting for something to come into her head.

After a while she found herself slipping into a slightly dreamy state, forgetting altogether about the problem of trying to write, just daydreaming really. And that was when she got her idea. It came to her almost like a picture in her head, the image of a girl staring out of a window at a rain-swept landscape and, after thinking about it for a little while, she began to write.

It was the story of a girl called Eliza. Her mother was dead, she had no brothers or sisters, and there were no other young women of her age living nearby. She lived a lonely life with only her rather grim father for company in a great big house in Cornwall.

She had got used to being by herself and had learned to accept that this was what her life would be like, when one day she met Mark, who worked in her father's mine. Mark had hardly any money and he certainly wasn't her social equal but he still managed to pluck up the courage to speak to her one day in the street and she admired him for that.

She and Mark struck up a friendship and they began to spend more and more time in each other's company, though this was something she kept from her father because she knew he would disapprove. Then, on her eighteenth birthday, her father gave her some terrible news. He had arranged for her to marry a man called George Dunwoody, who was twice her age, overweight and smelled like a horse. The very thought of him made Eliza shudder, but her father wasn't interested in her opinions.

When she told Mark about it that evening, he looked shocked. 'You can't marry him!' he said.

'What else can I do?' she demanded.

'Marry me!' he said. And that very night they made plans to run away together. Now she was sitting by her bedroom window in her father's house waiting for Mark's signal, a light shining in the darkness. But the appointed time had come and gone and there had been no sign from Mark. Eliza stared at the rain running endlessly down the window pane, wondering what on Earth could have happened to him.

Alice was pleased with what she had written. She had no idea how the story was going to end, but that didn't matter. She had enjoyed writing the description of Eliza staring mournfully out into the stormy night, waiting for something that would transform her life. She wasn't sure what Mr Carmody would think of it. Maybe it wasn't the sort of thing he wanted them to write, but this time at least, she had done more than just write a description of their timetable.

At twelve o'clock, Mr Carmody came round to tell them that it was their turn for lunch duty again. This time, however, Jasmine and Gary were in the group whose job it was to prepare the meal, while Alice and Matt were on clearing up duty. Jasmine went off, reluctantly, saying that she was sure other people were getting off more lightly than her. But Alice was pleased at the way it had worked out. She would have Matt to herself for a change.

Lunch was baked potatoes with grated cheese and salad, plus fruit or yoghurt. While they were eating, Mr Carmody announced that everyone could have the afternoon off.

'He makes it sound like we're being granted some big favour,' Gary said. 'The truth is, he's got no alternative because of the weather.'

'He's just trying to make the best of things,' Alice said.

Gary looked unimpressed. 'He should have planned things better.'

After everyone had finished eating, Alice and Matt began clearing up. They brought the dirty plates into the kitchen. Matt cleared away the uneaten food and handed the plates, one by one, to Alice who loaded them into the dishwasher.

'You know, you're really good on the guitar,' she told him while they worked.

'Thanks.'

'How long have you been playing?'

'Since I was ten.'

'Did you teach yourself?'

Matt shook his head. 'My dad taught me.'

'Is he a musician?'

'He used to be.'

'How come he isn't any more?'

Matt shrugged. 'Nowadays he's mostly just an alcoholic,' he said.

Alice was mortified. She had not expected an answer like this. She had just been trying to make conversation. She stood there with a dirty plate in her hand, wondering what she ought to say next. Finally she said, 'Sorry. I shouldn't have asked. It's none of my business.'

'It's OK,' Matt said. 'You weren't to know.'

Despite his assurance, Alice scolded herself for prattling like a child. She should have noticed that he was reluctant to answer her questions. Now she had embarrassed him. They continued to load the dishwasher in silence.

But it was Matt himself who brought the subject up again. 'When you were a kid, did you ever put your hand over a torch?' he asked.

'I'm not sure what you mean,' Alice said.

'Did you ever turn on a torch and then put your hand over it, so that the light shines through your fingers?'

'I don't think so,' Alice said.

'It makes your hand glow pink,' Matt said, 'a bit like something out of a science-fiction movie. Try it sometime. My dad used to do that when I was child. It was his little trick. He'd come up to my bedroom, sit beside the bed in the dark, turn on his torch and put his hand over the glass. Then he'd say to me, "That's what you've got to be like when you play guitar, like a light shining through skin and bone."

He was off his head, of course, but it made a big impression on me.'

Alice couldn't think what to say in reply. It was such a weird thing to tell her. Matt must have noticed her uncertainty because he laughed apologetically. 'I suppose you think I'm a bit crazy,' he said.

'No, I don't,' Alice told him. 'I think maybe your dad was right. After all, at least you've got something to aim for. I wish I had some sort of talent.'

'You do,' Matt told her.

'Like what?' Alice said. She knew he was trying to be nice but the truth was that she had no special talent. She was completely ordinary.

'You don't pretend,' Matt told her. 'You're not like the others. They just rush in and say what they think you want to hear, but you don't do that. You tell the truth. That's your talent.'

Alice caught her breath. No one had ever said anything like that to her before. Matt was looking directly at her and she looked back at him, wanting to thank him, but before she could open her mouth to speak Mr Carmody came into the kitchen, beaming heartily. 'How are you getting on with the dishes?' he asked.

'Nearly finished,' Matt told him.

'Good. You'll find the dishwasher powder in the cupboard under the sink. Just fill the container so that it's level, then switch the machine on. When you've done that, perhaps you could give the tables a wipe.' He continued to bustle around the kitchen, supervising them until everything was cleared away. There was no chance to continue their conversation.

They'd just finished when Jasmine appeared in the kitchen. 'One of the pool tables is free,' she said. 'Do you two fancy playing with Gary and me?'

Alice and Matt both agreed readily and they made their way to the recreation room where Gary had already set out the balls. 'OK,' he said when they were all standing round the table. 'We need to decide on teams. What about me and Alice versus Matt and Jasmine?'

Alice was just opening her mouth to say, why not the other way round: her and Matt versus Jasmine and Gary; but she couldn't think of a reason to give, other than the obvious one that she wanted to be with Matt.

While Alice was still thinking about it, Jasmine spoke first. 'OK!' she said. 'Let's toss a coin to see which team breaks.'

Alice's opportunity was gone.

Gary took a coin out of his pocket, flipped it in the

air and caught it. 'Heads or tails?' he asked Matt.

'Tails,' Matt said.

Gary opened his hand to show that he had caught the coin heads up. 'Alice and I break first,' he said.

It had all happened so quickly that there was absolutely nothing Alice could do about it. She was so annoyed, she could have snapped the cue that Gary handed her. 'Do you want to break or shall I?' he asked.

'You can,' Alice said, sullenly.

Gary broke and managed to get one of the balls in the pocket straight away. He looked very pleased with himself. 'Looks like you joined the winning team,' he told Alice cheerfully, but she took no notice. As far as she was concerned, she hadn't joined any team, she'd been bulldozed into it.

The others, however, were either unaware of her mood or else chose to ignore it. Jasmine seemed especially cheerful. 'Now you're going to see how it should be done,' she announced when Gary's go was over and it was Matt's turn.

However, Matt wasn't as skilled with the cue as he was with the guitar and it was soon Alice's turn. Still cross about what had happened, she hit the ball much too hard and sent it flying off the table altogether. The others all burst into laughter. Alice remained silent. She was wishing she hadn't agreed to play this stupid game.

'What was that you were saying a minute ago, Gary?' Jasmine asked.

'We've just got a few teething problems, that's all,' Gary said. 'Anyway it's your go next. Let's see how you make out.'

Jasmine bent over the table and lined up her cue with the ball, but before she could take her shot, Matt stopped her. 'You're not holding the cue properly,' he said. Standing behind her, he bent down and put his hands on hers. 'Like this,' he said.

Jasmine smiled and Alice felt certain that she was enjoying the lesson. She felt a hot current of anger rising up inside her. 'I don't want to play this game,' she said. Then, without waiting for any of them to reply, she put down her cue, turned round and walked out of the room.

She was angry with all of them, with Gary for constantly pestering her, with Jasmine for always taking charge of things and for trying to have Matt to herself, with Matt for making her think he was interested in her one minute and then practically putting his arms around Jasmine the next. And she was angry with herself for being so weak. She wanted to cry but she wouldn't let herself. Instead she lay on her bed in the dormitory, fighting back the tears as she remembered how, just for a moment, Matt had made her think she was someone special.

A moment later she heard the sound of the dormitory door being opened and Jasmine appeared. 'There you are,' she said, coming over to the bed. 'What happened?'

'I just didn't want to play any more,' Alice said. Then, when Jasmine continued to look at her, as if waiting for some sort of explanation, she added, 'I've got a headache.' As she said this, she remembered how Matt had said that she wasn't like the others, she told the truth. Yet here she was lying. She felt guilty about it but it was too difficult to talk about properly with Jasmine. She could not say that she was angry with her for letting Matt show her how to hold the pool cue. It would have sounded ridiculous.

'Gary was very disappointed when you left,' Jasmine said.

At this, Alice felt the anger flare up inside her again. 'Why do you keep going on about Gary all the time?' she demanded. 'I've told you I don't care what he thinks.'

'All right, all right,' Jasmine said. 'Keep your hair on. I can't help it if Gary fancies you, can I?'

'Well I don't fancy him, all right. I don't fancy anyone!'

Jasmine raised her eyebrows quizzically. 'So what are you going to do now?' she asked.

'Nothing,' Alice said.

'What, nothing at all?'

Alice shrugged. 'I just want to be left in peace,' she said.

'Please yourself,' Jasmine said. 'I was only trying to help.' She turned and walked away.

After she'd gone Alice felt bad. She knew she had acted like a spoilt brat but she hadn't been able to help herself. She lay on the bed with her eyes closed, regretting what had happened but powerless either to change it or even to forget about it. It was like the way she had felt when she had tried to describe herself, in her journal, as a piece of driftwood, tossed about on the waves, carried wherever the currents took her. She wondered whether anyone else had thoughts like this. Probably not. Probably other people could control what went on in their minds. They didn't make mountains out of molehills. As she lay there thinking this, she felt a sudden overwhelming desire to be at home, where people cared for her, where she was not just another student on the trip.

It was Ms Lucey who managed to drag her out of her depression. She came and found her about an hour later. 'Are you all right?' she asked. 'Somebody said you weren't feeling very well.'

'I'm OK now,' Alice said.

'Are you sure?'

'Yes.'

'Good. Well everyone's going to watch a video in the recreation room shortly,' she said. 'Mr Carmody went to the local video shop and hired one.'

'Oh, that was a good idea!' Alice said. 'What did he get?'

'He got a choice,' Ms Lucey told her. 'Everyone's voting on what they want to watch. Why don't you join them?'

'Thanks, I will.'

When Alice arrived, the others were all sitting in rows in the recreation room waiting for Mr Carmody to put on the video. Jasmine looked up as Alice got a chair and sat down beside her. 'How are you feeling?' she asked.

'I'm fine,' Alice said. 'Sorry about earlier on.'

'Forget it,' Jasmine replied.

One good thing about Jasmine, Alice decided as she sat waiting for the video, was that she didn't hold a grudge. She could easily have been stand-offish after the way Alice had behaved earlier. Plenty of others would have done so, but Jasmine just acted as if nothing had happened. Alice was grateful for that.

That evening after dinner, they had to read out their writing again. This time Alice felt more confident about what she had written and she sensed, from the reactions of the others, that they thought it was good. Several people commented on the description, which pleased her because that was the thing she was most proud of. Deenie, who was usually quiet but seemed to have a lot to say when it came to people's writing, said, 'I think Eliza is very passive.'

'That's an interesting point, Deenie,' Mr Carmody said. 'Would you like to expand on that a bit?'

'Well, I just mean that everything seems to happen to her,' Deenie said. 'I'd like to see her seizing the initiative in some way.'

Mr Carmody turned to Alice. 'Do you think that's possible?' he asked.

'I don't know,' Alice replied.

'Have you thought about what's going to happen next?' the teacher asked.

'I'm not sure,' Alice replied. 'But I think Eliza is going to have to face a hard choice.'

'Good,' Mr Carmody said. 'Choices are always

important milestones in stories. Right, let's move on to somebody else.'

Alice didn't notice much about what other people had written because she was so busy thinking about the question Mr Carmody had asked her. What would happen next in her story? Where was Mark, the young man Eliza was supposed to be running away with? Had something happened to him? Or had he changed his mind?

Alice was still thinking about her writing when she went to bed that night. Just before she fell asleep she made up her mind that Deenie was right. Eliza should be a more forceful character. She should take hold of her own fate. If Mark wasn't going to come and get her as he had promised, she should go out and find him.

That night she dreamt she was lost in a forest. She didn't know how she had got there, only that she had to find her way out. But there was no sign of any path, just a carpet of leaves underfoot and huge trees with smooth trunks like stone pillars on every side. She tried calling out for help but her voice was drowned by the sound of the wind, moaning through the tops of the trees.

It was the wind that finally woke her up. She opened her eyes to find that she had left the forest of her dreams behind but it was still the middle of the night and outside the wind was whistling round the hostel, shaking the glass in the windows. She had no idea what time it was but she had brought a little torch with her and it was on top of the cupboard beside the bed. She reached out her hand and felt for it. There it was. She switched it on and looked at her watch. It was two o'clock in the morning.

Then, recalling her conversation with Matt, she placed her left hand over the top of the torch. Immediately, she could see what he had meant. The light shone through the cracks between her fingers with a pink glow, as if it were shining through the skin itself. This then was what Matt was trying to achieve when he played guitar. But what did it mean? What was the light that shone through skin and bone? And then the answer came to her. It was your self. That was all. There was no need to pretend to be something you weren't, no need to worry about what other people thought about you. All you had to do was be yourself. And wasn't that what Matt had admired about her? Pleased with this thought, she switched off the torch, put it on top of the cupboard and went back to sleep.

9

Overnight, three people were killed in Germany when a bridge collapsed and in parts of France thousands of people were without electricity because high winds had brought power cables down. Mr Carmody told them this the next morning after breakfast. Of course, Britain was only experiencing the tail end of the storm, he pointed out. Nevertheless, the next twenty-four hours would be extremely wet and windy and, unfortunately, they would have to spend another day shut up in the hostel.

'Couldn't we go into a town and find some amusement arcades or something?' Gary suggested.

Mr Carmody shook his head. 'I certainly didn't bring you here to encourage you to get involved in gambling,' he replied. 'Besides, driving conditions are simply too bad. I'm sorry, I know it's spoiled the end of our trip, but I'm afraid that the weather is one thing we don't have any control over. So this morning we're going to look at a video.'

'Is it another film?' someone asked.

Mr Carmody shook his head. 'We're going to be watching a programme all about Cornwall and some of the famous people who've lived here.' There were groans at this. 'I'm sure you're going to find it very interesting,' he assured them.

'I'm sure we're not,' Jasmine said to Alice, quietly.

And she was right. The programme was thoroughly dull. It looked as if it had been made about twenty years earlier and the narrator had the weirdest accent Alice had ever heard. Afterwards, Mr Carmody made things worse by handing out printed questions about what they'd just watched. 'This is really scraping the bottom of the barrel,' Jasmine said, as they picked up their pens and began answering the questions.

By lunchtime Alice was bored stiff. She and Jasmine were sitting in the dining room talking about what they were going to do when they got back home, when Matt and Gary sat down opposite them.

'Enjoy the morning?' Gary asked.

'Loved it,' Jasmine replied.

Gary looked quickly round the room, then he lowered his voice. 'We're thinking of going out later,' he said.

'Where?' Alice asked.

Gary shrugged. 'Anywhere. I'm getting cabin fever cooped up in here.

'What are you going to do?'

He leaned even closer towards them. Then he whispered, 'I've got a bit of dope. Don't tell anyone else, though. OK?'

The two girls nodded.

'We're going to go out and have a spliff some time this afternoon,' he went on. 'Are you two up for it?'

Jasmine grinned enthusiastically. 'Definitely,' she said.

'What about you, Alice?' Gary asked.

Alice glanced at Matt. She got the feeling that he was waiting to see what she would say. She nodded her head. 'Count me in.'

'OK. We'll let you know when we're going.'

After lunch, Mr Carmody announced that he wanted everyone to concentrate on their writing. There were more groans at this. Everyone clearly felt that they'd done enough writing. But Mr Carmody was adamant. So, with a great deal of discontented muttering, the students moved off to find themselves spots where they could work. Alice chose a table in a corner of the dining room and set to work on her story.

It was hard to get back into Eliza's mind at first, so Alice closed her eyes and tried to concentrate. To begin with, all she could think about was the sound of the rain battering against the windows but gradually she began to conjure up the world of her story. There, too, the weather had worsened but Eliza continued to stare out into the night, straining her eyes for a glimmer of light in the darkness. And then, just when she was beginning to give up all hope, she saw it.

Alice opened her eyes, picked up her pen and began to write. She described how Eliza went quickly upstairs to her bedroom, put on her coat and hat and came back down into the hall. Then she tiptoed past her father's study and stole out the front door as quietly as she could.

Outside the storm was raging and Eliza was almost swept off her feet as she forced her way against the wind, heading in the direction of the light. She was wet through before she finally reached the shelter of the trees. As she called Mark's name, her voice seemed to be snatched away by the wind. Then from the shadow of the trees a figure stepped forwards. Joyfully she turned to greet her lover, but it was not Mark. It was George Dunwoody, smiling coldly at her.

'Alice?'

Startled, she looked up to see Gary, Jasmine and Matt. She had been so caught up in writing her story that she had not seen them approach.

'Are you coming?'

Alice glanced out the window. It was raining harder than ever. 'Where are we going to go?' she asked. 'It's pouring out there.'

'There's some sort of tool shed round the back of the hostel,' Gary said. 'I noticed it the day we went to Belmouth. It's only got a bolt on the door so we should be able to get inside. But we'd better not all go together. It's too obvious. Matt and I will go first. You two follow in a couple of minutes.'

'OK.'

Alice felt excited and just a little bit scared as she watched Gary and Matt slip away. There was no doubt they would all be in trouble if they got caught and she wasn't used to being in trouble. She wasn't that sort of girl. Normally she just kept her head down and got on with things. But she told herself that you couldn't always be good.

'Come on, then,' Jasmine said, when a few minutes had passed. 'Let's go and get our coats, otherwise we're going to get soaked.'

Fortunately, the teachers were all shut up in the office and most of the students were busy with their writing as Alice and Jasmine made their way to the dormitory. They bundled up their coats, making them as small as possible, and crammed them into a plastic carrier bag. At the last minute, Alice decided to take her scarf as well. Then they went back to the foyer and, when they were sure that no one was watching, slipped quickly out of the front door.

The rain lashed at them the moment they stepped outside and they quickly struggled into their coats. In the process, the plastic carrier bag was whipped out of Alice's hands and sailed away on the wind.

'Leave it,' Jasmine said, as Alice made an effort to retrieve it. 'Come on, quickly, before someone sees us.'

They ran around the side of the building, bending down almost on all fours as they made their way past the windows. They had no difficulty finding the shed that Gary had described and there was Matt's face peering out at them through the window.

Jasmine opened the door, the two girls squeezed inside and pulled the door shut behind them, giggling. It was dark inside and dusty and there were cobwebs in the corners. The place seemed to be used mostly for storing old furniture. A lot of plastic chairs and several metal tables were stacked at the back. Gary was bending over one of these busily rolling a joint. He looked up when they came in. 'Are you sure nobody saw you?' he asked.

'Certain,' Jasmine told him.

'Good. Well just keep a lookout while I roll this spliff, will you?'

While Gary busied himself with the cigarette papers, tobacco and dope, the rain beat an incessant rhythm on the corrugated steel roof of the shed and the wind raged outside. Alice stood beside Matt and peered out at a little clump of trees nearby which were bending and swaying as if they were alive. There wasn't a lot of spare room in the shed and she was very conscious of the fact that, as they stood beside each other, their legs brushed together. She wondered whether he too was aware of this, and, if so, what he thought about it.

'Right, that should do,' Gary said. He held up the joint for them to see. 'At least some people had the sense to bring a little alternative entertainment with them,' he said. 'Unlike Mr Carmody, I thought ahead.'

'Just light it, Gary,' Matt said.

'Patience,' Gary replied. He put the joint in his mouth, took a lighter out of his pocket and lit the end. He sucked deeply, then blew out a cloud of smoke. 'Perfect!'

'God, that smells really strong!' Jasmine said.

'It's skunk,' Gary told her. 'It smells strong because it is strong.' He passed the joint to Matt, who took a couple of drags and handed it to Alice.

She put it to her lips and drew in the smoke. It was hot and acrid and she breathed in much more smoke than she had intended. She burst into a fit of coughing. 'It hurts my throat,' she complained. Gary only giggled at her, which annoyed her so much that she pulled herself together and tried again, more gently. This time she found she was able to hold the smoke in, before blowing it out again in a long stream. She passed the joint to Jasmine.

It went round twice more before Gary stubbed it out and by that time Alice was really beginning to feel the effect. The first thing she noticed was how weird things were looking. The dusty old shed in which they had been standing seemed to have been transformed, as if someone had sprinkled it with fairy dust, so that the angles and shadows made by the stacks of old furniture were somehow intriguing and full of possibilities. And her friends, too, seemed different. She looked into their faces as if she was seeing them for the first time. It struck her that there was something almost animal-like about Gary. He reminded her of some big bird, like an eagle. Jasmine, on the other hand, looked younger than she remembered, like a little girl, which was strange because usually Alice tended to look up to her. Now it seemed to her that there was something quite vulnerable, almost fragile about her friend. Matt, however, looked older and even more good-looking than she had always thought him. There was something magnetic about him, as if he drew in energy, and Alice was suddenly aware of just how attracted she was to him.

'Wow! This stuff is strong,' Jasmine said. 'I can feel it in my arms and legs.'

'What do they feel like?' Alice asked.

'Sort of tingly,' Jasmine told her. She began to giggle and for no particular reason, except for the fact that she had sneaked out of the hostel without anyone noticing and was now standing in a shed in the wilds of Cornwall feeling excited and happy, Alice found herself joining in. Soon all four of them were giggling uncontrollably and it seemed that they would never be able to stop. Alice made a big effort, closed her eyes and pulled herself together. But as soon as she opened her eyes again and caught sight of Jasmine's face, she burst out laughing anew, which made the others laugh even more.

It was Matt who brought them back down to Earth. He stopped laughing and seemed to be listening. 'Listen to the sound of the wind,' he said.

They listened. He was right. It was an extraordinary sound, so full of power and energy, that Alice wanted to run out into the night and let it take her wherever it wanted.

'It's beautiful,' Jasmine said.

'You know what would be really cool?' Gary suggested.

'What?'

'If we went down to the sea right now. I bet the waves would be amazing.'

Alice opened her mouth to say that maybe this wasn't such a good idea, that they might be missed back at the hostel, but she glanced at Jasmine and saw that her face had lit up at the suggestion. There was a slightly manic look in her eye. 'Let's do it,' Jasmine said.

Gary glanced at the others.

'I'm up for it,' Matt said.

All three of them looked at Alice. She hesitated. 'OK,' she agreed.

Gary opened the door of the shed and the four of them went outside. The sky was a weird yellow colour and Alice felt as if she were stepping back in time to the beginnings of the world, so wild and furious was the weather. But she also felt an answering response deep inside her, as if some hidden part of her had been stirred up by the elements, some instinct that she had almost forgotten she possessed, a feeling of oneness with nature. This must be what it's like to be a wild animal, she told herself.

They made their way towards the path that led down to the sea, taking care to remain out of sight of the hostel. Gary went first, Jasmine followed close behind, then came Matt and Alice. As they walked, Alice found herself drawing closer to Matt. There was something about being near him that made her feel safe, even though all around them a storm was raging. He did not want to lead all the time, like Gary, but he seemed to possess an inner confidence.

She felt very different now that she was outside, less affected by the dope in some ways, more affected in others. Inside the shed, she had felt as if they were closeted together in some sort of Aladdin's cave and it had seemed that the world around her had changed in some subtle, indefinable way. Now she was more focused on the way she felt herself, her physical sensations – the feeling of the rain on her skin, the wind blowing through her hair. And she was especially conscious of an increasing desire to reach out and take Matt's hand, to feel his strength flowing into her body from the contact.

Gary and Jasmine were a little way ahead of them when the wind snatched at Alice's scarf. It flew out behind her, catching on some barbed-wire fencing. Alice was taken aback by the force of the wind, the way it had just ripped the scarf from around her neck and flung it on to the fence. Laughing, she went over to retrieve it, but it wasn't easy because the scarf seemed to be caught in so many places and each time she released one part of it, the wind blew it back on to the fence. Then Matt glanced back and saw what had happened. He came over to help and together they peeled the scarf off the wire.

'Thanks,' Alice said.

'That's OK.' He was standing right beside her now and as she stared at him she saw that there was a different look on his face – a look of intense concentration, as if he was trying to say something but couldn't quite put it into words. A moment later, he bent his head toward hers and began to kiss her.

It took her completely by surprise, even though it was what she had wanted for such a long time. Over Matt's shoulder, she caught a glimpse of Jasmine's face looking back at them and she felt a little thrill of triumph. It seemed to Alice that Jasmine looked shocked, though maybe that was just her guilty conscience. But why should I have a guilty conscience? she asked herself. All's fair in love and war. And she was quite sure that if it had been Jasmine that Matt had chosen, she wouldn't have turned him down. Anyway, she wasn't going to dwell on the matter. Instead, she closed her eyes and concentrated on kissing Matt back.

Although she would never have admitted it to anyone else, it was the first time she had kissed a boy properly. Now that she had started, she didn't want to stop. The whole of her attention was focused on the act as she felt his tongue sliding into her mouth and his body pressing against hers. Deep inside her, she was aware of something kindling into life. Like a serpent uncoiling fold by fold, pleasure was beginning to make its way through her body. All around them the wind continued to rage, but they were completely unaware of it, seeming to melt into each other so that they were more like one creature than two separate people.

Afterwards, when she tried to remember how long they had stood there, Alice could not be sure. It had seemed to her to be just one big long 'now', as if time had folded in on itself and created a space around them quite separate from the outside world. Maybe it was five minutes, maybe it was longer. All Alice could say for certain was that it ended when she became aware of shouting. She broke away from Matt, opened her eyes and caught sight of Gary in the distance, running towards them as fast as his legs would carry him and calling out something incoherent.

In that instant, she knew that something utterly terrible had happened. She felt shock hit her like a wall of flame and stood there, unable to speak, as Gary came panting up to them. 'What's the matter?' Matt asked him.

'It's Jasmine,' he said blankly.

'What about her?'

'She was standing on the sea wall. Then this huge wave came over the top and the next second she was gone.'

'What do you mean – gone?'

'She was washed off the top of the wall into the water. There wasn't anything I could do to save her.'

10

For a moment both Alice and Matt were paralysed by the horror of what they had just heard. They stood staring at Gary, unable even to speak. It was Alice who was the first one to come to her senses. 'We've got to get help,' she said. 'We've got to tell Mr Carmody.'

Now Matt sprang to life. 'I'll go back to the hostel and tell them what happened,' he said. 'You two go down to the water and try to see where she is.' Then he turned and began running as quickly as he could back towards the hostel.

It seemed so much further down to the water than when they had all cheerfully walked down the path on their first day, but at last they came out beside the rock wall that overlooked the sea. They called Jasmine's name over and over again but their voices sounded completely insignificant against the roar of the wind and the waves. There was no response, nor could they see any sign of her. Even as they stood there, gazing desperately out to sea, a huge wave came crashing up against the cliff face, sending a plume of spray high over the top of the wall. Alice instinctively stepped backwards. She found herself wondering why on Earth Jasmine had been standing on top of the wall when only two days ago she had been too frightened to climb the rock face under the guidance of professional tutors.

But there was no time for questions like that now. Somewhere in the freezing, grey water below them, Jasmine was struggling to stay afloat. They had to keep scanning the water, to see if they could locate her. For what seemed like forever, they strained their eyes against the wind and the rain. Then suddenly Gary shouted out, 'There she is!'

'Where?'

'Over there! Look!'

Alice looked in the direction he pointed but at first she could see nothing. Then, much further out than she had expected, she noticed a tiny figure, bobbing up and down in the water.

'Oh my God!' Alice said. 'She's so far out!'

Perhaps Jasmine could see them because just at that moment she raised an arm above her head. Then, as abruptly as she had appeared, she disappeared again beneath a huge wave.

'Where is she now?' Alice said, frantically. 'I can't see her any more.'

'Neither can I,' Gary said. 'But she must be there somewhere. We just have to keep looking.'

Desperately, they sought to catch another glimpse of that doll-like shape tossed about on the water, but there was no sign of her. The waves continued to crash against the side of the cliff, soaking them both with spray. Alice began shaking with cold and shock and crying silently at the thought of her friend, who only half an hour ago had been giggling like a child at a birthday party, but was now struggling to stay afloat in that vast, hostile sea while ice-cold water gnawed at her bones.

'Get back!' A voice behind them barked. It was Mr Carmody and Ms Lucey was with him. Ms Lucey took hold of Alice's arm and pulled her back from the sea wall. She hadn't realised how close to the edge they'd been standing.

'Have you seen her?' Ms Lucey asked.

'Yes,' Gary said. 'We saw her over there a few minutes ago.' He pointed.

'She was ever such a long way out,' Alice said. 'But she was waving at us, so I think she must have seen us. Then we lost sight of her.'

'All right,' Mr Carmody said. 'I want you to go

back to the hostel now with Ms Lucey. The rescue services will be here shortly.

'They will be able to save her, won't they?' Alice said.

Mr Carmody nodded. 'I'm sure they will, Alice. Now both of you go back to the hostel immediately. We don't want any more accidents.'

It seemed dreadful to turn her back on Jasmine and walk away but that was what she had to do. Mr Carmody and Ms Lucey were insistent. On the way back to the hostel, Ms Lucey asked them to describe how the accident had happened.

'When we got down to the sea wall, Jasmine said she was going to chase away her demons,' Gary told her.

'What did she mean by that?'

'She meant she wanted to overcome her fear of heights, I think. That's why she climbed on top of the wall. She was dancing about and calling out, "I can do it, I can do it".'

Alice could picture the scene: Jasmine with that manic look in her eye, waving her arms above her head in triumph, as if by overcoming her own nature, she could control the world around her.

'Didn't you try to stop her?' Ms Lucey asked.

'I told her to be careful, but she wouldn't take any

notice of me. Then this massive wave came crashing over the top of the wall and it just swept her away. It happened so quickly. There was nothing I could do about it.'

'I don't understand what the four of you were doing outside, anyway,' Ms Lucey said. 'You were told to stay in the hostel.'

'We wanted to go for a walk.'

'In the middle of a storm?'

'I know it was a stupid thing to do.'

'It was more than stupid, Gary,' Ms Lucey told him, grimly.

'How long will the rescue people be?' Alice asked.

'They'll be launching a lifeboat any minute now,' Ms Lucey replied. 'You know, Alice, I'm surprised at you. I thought you had more sense than to get involved in something like this.'

Alice hung her head. 'I'm sorry miss,' she said.

'It's not much good being sorry now, is it?'

When they got back to the hostel, Alice and Gary were made to change their clothes and dry themselves. The other students had been assembled in the dining hall where Ms Wilkinson was taking a register. As Alice walked past the doorway, all the heads turned and everyone's eyes looked in her direction. Like I'm some sort of monster, Alice thought.

She and Gary were told to wait in the teachers' common room, where Matt was already sitting. 'Did you see her?' he asked, as soon as they walked in.

'Yes,' Alice said. 'Then we lost sight of her again.'

'You didn't tell them about the dope, did you?' Gary asked.

Matt shook his head.

Alice looked at Gary in disgust. 'Is that all you can think about?' she asked.

'Of course not,' Gary said. 'I just wanted to know.'

Ms Lucey came back then with blankets and mugs of hot, sweet tea, which she told them was good for shock. Alice drank hers without really tasting it. Ms Lucey told them that the lifeboat had been launched a few miles up the coast and would be in the area within minutes.

After a while Mr Carmody returned. At first, Alice felt a surge of hope when she saw him, but he shook his head when she asked if there was any news. 'Everything is being done that can be done,' he said. Then he disappeared again.

Not long after that, they heard the sound of a helicopter overhead. They listened as the sound drew nearer then faded away again. 'They'll find her,' Gary said. The other two said nothing.

The next time a teacher appeared it was Ms

Lucey to say that the police had arrived and that they wanted to interview Alice, Gary and Matt separately. She asked the boys to come with her. 'Alice, you stay here,' she said. 'The police will come and speak to you in a minute.'

The two boys followed Ms Lucey out of the room. As Gary passed Alice, he gave her a beseeching look. Alice knew what he was trying to convey to her – he wanted her to keep quiet about the dope – but she made no response. She had not made up her mind yet what she would tell the police.

Ms Lucey came back a few minutes later with two officers – a woman and a man. The man was very tall, middle-aged with dark hair and heavy eyebrows. The woman was smaller and younger with short blonde hair and thin lips. She was the one who did most of the talking. She spoke gently with a strong Cornish accent and her colleague made notes.

'What's your name?' she began.

'Alice Marsden.'

'How old are you, Alice?'

'Sixteen.'

'Right. Now I know this may be distressing for you, but I need you to describe what happened this afternoon, in your own words. OK?'

Alice nodded. 'We went for a walk.'

'Who went on this walk, exactly?'

'Me and Jasmine and Gary and Matt.'

'And what time was this?'

'I'm not sure,' Alice said. She seemed to have lost all sense of time. She tried to remember how long ago it had been. 'About an hour ago, I think.'

'OK, so you decided to go for a walk. Had it been pointed out to you that there was a storm in progress?'

'Yes.'

'And had you been given any instructions about going outside?'

'We were told not to.'

'By whom?'

'Mr Carmody.'

'That's your teacher?'

'Yes.'

'He definitely told you that you shouldn't go outside?'

'Yes.'

'But you chose to disregard that instruction?'

'Yes.'

'Why did you do that?'

Alice shrugged. 'I don't know. We were fed up with being inside, I suppose.'

'Did you tell anyone about what you were doing,

any of the other students, for example?'

'No.'

'OK. So you left the building. What happened next?'

'We decided to go down to the sea, to look at the waves. Because we thought they'd be spectacular. But Matt and I got separated from the other two.'

'How did that happen?'

'My scarf got tangled in the fence and Matt helped me untangle it.'

'The others didn't wait for you?'

Alice hesitated. Finally she said, 'We were kissing.'

The policewoman nodded. 'I see. OK, so you got separated. Carry on.'

'The other two went down to the sea by themselves and then a few minutes later Gary came running back, shouting that Jasmine had fallen into the water. I ran down to the sea with him to look for her and Matt ran back to the hostel to get help.'

'You didn't see how the accident happened then?'

'No.'

'All right, thank you. We may have to ask you some more questions later on, but that will do for now.'

Alice stood up. Her legs were shaking and she felt

as if they might give way beneath her at any moment. Ms Lucey led her into the dining room, where the other students were still sitting at the tables. There was a hush when she came in.

'OK, Alice. I'm going to leave you here,' Ms Lucey said. She was speaking quite gently now, as if she was talking to an infant. Her voice had lost the coldness that it had possessed earlier. 'Are you going to be all right?' she asked.

Alice nodded. She sat down on a chair against the wall, apart from the other students. She didn't feel that she could join them, not after what had happened.

'You promise you're not going to leave the building again?'

'I promise.'

'And you won't do anything silly?'

'No miss.'

'OK.' Ms Lucey turned to Phoebe. 'Phoebe, I want you to keep an eye on Alice for me. Will you do that?'

'Yes, miss.'

'Thank you.'

Phoebe came and sat down next to Alice. She put her arm round her. 'They'll find her,' she said, echoing the words that Gary had used earlier. Alice badly wanted to believe it. She desperately needed some sort of comfort, some hope that she could cling to. But into her mind came the memory of that tiny, doll-like figure waving an arm above her head before disappearing beneath the waves.

'People can survive for longer than you think in the sea,' Phoebe said. 'And the rescue people know what they're doing. They're experienced at this kind of thing.'

'She was such a long way out, though,' Alice said.

'They'll rescue her,' Phoebe repeated. 'I know they will. You mustn't give up hope.'

There was nothing to do then but wait and wish, over and over again, that they had stayed inside the hostel like everyone else. She thought about the questions the police had asked her and the fact that she hadn't told them the whole story. Would they find out what had really happened? And, if so, would she be in trouble for not mentioning the dope? Perhaps she should have told the whole truth. Hadn't Matt said that this was her special talent? Maybe she ought to go back and tell them everything right now. She stood up, on the point of doing exactly that. But then she hesitated and sat down again.

'What's the matter?' Phoebe asked.

Alice shook her head. 'Nothing,' she said. What good would it do to? she asked herself. It wouldn't help them find Jasmine more quickly. It wouldn't make the sea any less cold or any less deep.

As she sat there thinking this, Matt came into the room. He looked at her, as if he would have liked to say something, but then went and sat down instead. He put his head on the table in front of him and closed his eyes, shutting out the rest of the world.

A little while later, Gary joined them. He too sat down without a word and gnawed at his fingernails. He was white-faced and there was something about him that reminded Alice of an animal in a trap.

Mr Carmody reappeared then and announced that a second lifeboat had joined the search. He was trying to sound hopeful but his expression was that of a man who was living through a nightmare. 'The school has contacted all your parents,' he went on. 'So I'd like you to phone home now and reassure them that you're safe. If anyone hasn't got a mobile phone with them, then please come and see me, Ms Lucey or Ms Wilkinson and we'll lend you one.'

As soon as he'd finished speaking, Alice's phone rang.

It was her mother. 'Alice, it's Mum. Are you all right?' she asked.

The sound of her mother's voice was enough to make Alice start crying once more. 'I'm not all right,' she sobbed. 'I'm never going to be all right again, Mum.'

Her mother was saying something on the other end of the line, but Alice couldn't hear properly. 'Just a minute,' she said. She put down the phone, blew her nose and made an effort to pull herself together. 'Sorry about that,' she said, when she had picked up the phone again.

'That's all right. It must be terrible for you.'

'It doesn't matter about me,' Alice replied. 'It's Jasmine, Mum, they're not going to find her.'

'I'm sure they will, darling. They know what they're doing.'

'Yes but it's been nearly two hours now and it's freezing out there.'

'You mustn't give up hope. Everyone's praying for her.'

'I've been praying, too,' Alice told her. 'But it hasn't done any good.'

'You don't know that yet. Listen, I'm going to put your dad on now. He wants to say a few words.'

'OK.'

Her father came on the line then. He repeated the same things that her mother had said: that the rescue workers would find Jasmine soon, that they had lots of experience and that she shouldn't give up hope. Then he handed the phone back to her mother. 'I want you to phone us at any time of the day or night, if you need to talk,' she told Alice.

'OK, Mum. Thanks.'

'I wish I was there with you.'

'I wish you were here too.'

'Listen, take care of yourself, darling, and we'll see you very soon.'

'OK.'

'We love you, Alice.'

'I love you too, Mum.'

Dinner was prepared by the hostel staff and the students queued up for it listlessly. Alice didn't want to bother with food but Ms Lucey brought a plate with a portion of chicken, potatoes and some peas over to the table where she was sitting. 'I want you to try and eat,' she told Alice. 'There's no point in making yourself ill. That won't help Jasmine, will it?'

Alice nodded. She tried to eat some of the food but it was like packing tissues into her mouth. Nothing had any taste. She moved her jaws up and down mechanically but her mouth seemed to be completely dry and it was an effort to swallow.

'How long has it been now?' Matt asked. She had not even realised that he and Gary had sat down at the same table.

'Nearly three hours,' Gary told him.

'There's still time,' Matt said.

Alice didn't want to hear them speculate about how long Jasmine might be able to survive. She pushed her plate away, got up and went to the dormitory, where she threw herself down on the bed. But, even here, there was no peace because right beside her was Jasmine's empty bed, a visible reminder of what had happened to her friend. Into her mind came the memory of Jasmine handing her the fossil wrapped in tissue paper on the morning of her birthday. Was that really only the day before yesterday? Suddenly, she recalled the words of the poem that the fossil had inspired, the description of someone drifting down through icy water with their mouth wide open, calling for help without once disturbing the silence. It was such a shocking image that she sat up on the bed and clutched her head in her hands, pulling at her hair as hard as she could, as if the pain would somehow purge the picture from her mind. But it was no good. She could still see it ever so clearly. And it was not some nameless sailor slipping down into the freezing depth but Jasmine, her best friend, the girl who had made her feel welcome when she had been a stranger at school, who had spoken to her when no one else was interested, the friend whose bedroom she had slept in, with whom she had been to parties and who had been her rival for Matt's affection.

That last thought was like a knife being turned in a wound. She remembered the way she had resented Jasmine's presence when Matt was around and the little sense of triumph she had felt when Jasmine had seen them kissing. What kind of a friend had she been? The very worst kind, she decided, the kind who acts pleased to see someone but secretly does everything they can to undermine them.

Alice had never prayed in her life before today. In fact, if she had been asked whether or not she believed in God she probably would have said no. But ever since Gary had come rushing back from the sea with the news about Jasmine, she had found herself saying over and over again to someone or something, 'Please let her be all right, please let them find her.' Now she promised that if her prayer was answered, she would be a better person in future. She'd be honest about things, like

Matt had said she was, she wouldn't keep her resentments to herself, letting them fester away under the surface.

But if God was listening, he wasn't answering. There was just a terrible emptiness inside her and the constant drip, drip, drip of her own guilt like a leaking tap in an empty building.

11

When Alice got off the bed and wandered back to join the others, she found them sitting in the recreation room watching the news. The newsreader was describing how coastguard services, assisted by an RAF helicopter, were searching for a sixteen-year-old girl who had been washed out to sea. There were pictures of the helicopter hovering over a very rough sea, while the newsreader explained that the rescue attempt was being hindered by adverse weather conditions. That was all he said. Then he moved on to an item about plans to build a caravan park in the face of opposition from local residents.

Not long after that, a camera crew turned up at the hostel and, though the hostel staff turned them away, they stood outside, filming the building. Mr Carmody called everyone together. 'You're probably aware that the media have arrived,' he said. 'We've given them a statement that has been agreed with the school, but we don't believe that talking to them further will help the situation at the moment. We've got to remember that this is an extremely difficult time for Jasmine's parents and we don't want anyone saying anything that might add to their distress. So, if you are contacted by somebody you don't know and asked about the situation, I'd be very grateful if you'd refrain from speaking about it. And, of course, I want to repeat what you've already been told before. No one is to leave the building unless they are specifically told to do so by myself or one of the other teachers. OK, now Ms Wilkinson is going to read a prayer for Jasmine's return.'

Ms Wilkinson held up a piece of paper and began to read aloud a prayer for Jasmine's safety and guidance for the men and women who were searching for her. Alice joined in the chorus of amens afterwards but, in her heart, she could not help feeling that it would do no good.

The evening wore on with unbearable slowness. It was like watching the sand trickle through an enormous hour glass, grain by grain. And with every minute that passed, the likelihood of Jasmine's rescue got further and further away. Mr Carmody and Ms Wilkinson spent most of the time shut up in the office making phone calls. Ms Lucey went around talking to individual students, trying to reassure them. A little knot of reporters stayed camped outside the gates of the hostel, waiting to see what would happen.

'They're like vultures around a wounded animal,' Matt said.

Alice shrugged. 'I suppose they've got a job to do,' she replied.

'It's not a job I'd fancy,' he said. 'Scenting out other people's distress.'

'Stuff like this appears on the news all the time,' Alice told him, 'and you don't take any notice of it, because you never believe it's going to happen to you. Then one day it does.'

Matt turned away from the window. 'Why do you think she climbed on to the wall?' he asked.

'Because she wanted to be brave, like Gary said.'

'But she wouldn't even attempt the Wedge with the rest of us.'

'That's the point. She wanted to prove something. Anyway, let's face it, none of us were behaving very sensibly.'

Matt looked at her for a long time after she said this. Finally he said, 'Is that what you think?'

'Of course it is.'

'Maybe you're right.' He got up and wandered away, leaving Alice by herself again. Only much later, when she was back in Beckerton, did she realise that her answer had been hurtful. But on that day she thought nothing of it. Instead she went back to doing what she had been doing ever since the accident had happened – replaying the events of the afternoon and thinking of all the points at which things could have turned out differently. If only Gary hadn't suggested that they go outside to smoke the dope. If only they hadn't agreed to go. And if only he had not come up with the stupid idea that they go down to the sea. She could remember the delighted way in which he had suggested it. 'You know what would be really cool?' he'd said. Well it hadn't turned out to be very cool, had it?

She was angry with Gary, but she was also angry with herself because she could have spoken up and said it was too dangerous. And the truth was that this thought had briefly come into her mind, while she had stood in the shed, hesitating for an instant. It had been like a candle flame flickering in the darkness of her mind, but she had deliberately ignored it, snuffed out the warning because she had wanted to be with the others, and in particular – with Matt. That was what she felt worst about. Because if she and Matt had not started kissing, then maybe, just maybe, Jasmine would not have felt quite such a need to prove herself. That was what she had been doing after all, trying to claw back a little pride. Whenever she reached this point in her thoughts Alice remembered again, with shame, the little feeling of triumph she had experienced when she had glimpsed Jasmine's shocked face over Matt's shoulder.

She told herself that it didn't help to think like this, that no matter how much she wanted to, she could not go back in time and change what had happened. But, at the same time, another voice inside her kept insisting that this whole thing could have been avoided if she had not been so passive, like the girl in the story she had written. If she had listened to the instinct that had told her it was madness to go down to the sea in the middle of a storm, she could have taken charge of the situation.

She should have realised that life was not something that just happened to you and that a tragedy was not just a sudden scream. It was a long complicated chain of events, each following on from the one before. At any point, that chain could have been broken and she could have been the one to break it.

12

All night long in her dreams Alice kept returning to the moment when Gary had come running along the path shouting something unintelligible about Jasmine. Over and over again she broke off from kissing Matt and listened to the news that her friend had fallen into the water. Or else she stood behind the sea wall staring hopelessly out to sea, then catching a glimpse of Jasmine before she disappeared beneath the waves.

Once she sat up in the darkness, wide awake, convinced that she had heard Jasmine whispering her name. She was so certain that it had been real, she reached for her torch and shone it all around the dormitory, but there was no one there, just a room full of sleeping girls and, beside her, Jasmine's empty bed. She switched off the torch and lay back down again, reluctant to return to a sleep which offered no peace, no forgetfulness and no refuge.

But despite her resistance, sleep crept over her

once more and the next time she awoke it was morning and Ms Lucey was standing in her usual place between the two rows of beds, telling them that it was time to get up.

Alice sat up in bed and looked at Ms Lucey's face, hoping to see some sign that all was well after all, that during the night Jasmine had somehow miraculously been discovered. But there was no glimmer of hope about Ms Lucey's expression, only the same weary resignation. It's still true then, she thought. Nevertheless, she had to hear it confirmed.

'Miss, has there been any news?' she asked.

Ms Lucey shook her head. 'I'm afraid not, Alice,' she said. 'The search has continued all night but they haven't found her.'

The dormitory, which was usually so full of chatter and laughter first thing in the morning, was almost empty of sound as the girls dressed and made their way to the dining room in silence. It felt to Alice as though all the colour had been drained out of the world so that everything around her was grey and empty of life. She would have liked to lie back down on the bed and fall asleep again in the hope that she might wake up in a different world, one that had not had the heart ripped out of it. But there was no avoiding the truth. She got out of bed, pulled on her clothes and followed the others.

Breakfast was cereal and toast. The blinds were drawn in the dining room, in case the photographers and cameramen, who had grown in number overnight, thought it worth their while to take pictures of the students eating their breakfast. Alice took a bowl of cereal and tried to force some down but it tasted like wet leaves. She put the bowl aside and sipped some tea instead. It was so hot that it burnt her tongue, but she didn't care. In fact she welcomed the pain. At least it was something different to focus on.

When they were all sitting down, Mr Carmody gave them a talk. He told them what they already knew, that there had been no progress in the search for Jasmine and, though he stressed that there was still hope, it was clear he didn't believe it. Neither did anyone else in the room. Throughout the hours of darkness, while they had been sleeping, the rescue services had continued to patrol the waters, the beam of the helicopter's lamp cutting a swathe of light through the darkness, but they had found nothing except cold grey water. Soon, they would begin scaling down the search in the knowledge that no one could survive, unprotected, in the sea for so many hours.

After breakfast, Alice's mother rang again. She'd already spoken to the school and learned that there was no news but was still trying to sound hopeful. She tried to convince Alice that Jasmine could have been washed ashore somewhere further up the coast and that she still might be discovered alive. But it didn't sound very likely to Alice and she could tell from her mother's voice that she did not really believe it herself.

At half past ten, Ms Wilkinson drove to the nearest railway station to meet Jasmine's parents, who had caught the first train that morning down from London. She returned about an hour later. Alice watched through the window as they got out of the car, moving slowly and stiffly, their faces looking as if they were carved out of stone. As soon as she saw them, Alice felt the urge to run away and hide. She dreaded the thought of having to face them and talk about what had happened. But there was no avoiding it. A little while later Ms Lucey came and found her. 'Alice, Jasmine's mum and dad have asked if they could speak to you,' she said.

Alice nodded. She got up and followed Ms Lucey.

Jasmine's parents were sitting in the office with Mr Carmody. They looked haggard and it was clear that Jasmine's mother had been crying. 'Hello

Alice,' she said.

'Hello,' Alice said. She stood uncertainly by the door. In the past she had always felt quite relaxed in the presence of Jasmine's parents, but now she didn't know what to do with herself.

'Sit down, Alice,' Mr Carmody told her. 'Mrs and Mrs Hayes wanted to ask you a few questions about Jasmine. They know you weren't there when the accident actually happened, but they wanted to talk to you because you're Jasmine's best friend and they thought you might be able to help them understand things a little bit better. OK?'

Alice nodded. She sat down and waited to hear what they would say.

'Alice,' Jasmine's father said, 'what we really wanted to ask about was Jasmine's mood.' He spoke slowly as if he was having difficulty finding the words. 'What I mean is, how did Jasmine seem to you?'

'How did she seem?' Alice repeated, unsure what she should answer.

'Was she upset about anything – or depressed? That's what we want to know,' Jasmine's mother interrupted. 'Because we wouldn't want to think...' She stopped, unable to say any more.

Alice realised that they were trying to ask her

whether what had happened had really been an accident. She shook her head. 'No, Mrs Hayes,' she said, 'I'm sure she wasn't upset about anything. In fact, she was feeling really happy. We all were.'

'Then I don't understand why she would do such a stupid thing,' her mother went on. 'She's normally such a sensible girl.'

'She wasn't really thinking,' Alice said. 'None of us were. We were having a good time and we just got carried away.'

Jasmine's father nodded. 'Then she didn't have a quarrel with anyone?'

'No.'

'But what was she doing climbing up on this wall? It doesn't make sense.' Jasmine's mother still looked at Alice in bewilderment.

'I think she was trying to overcome her fear of heights,' Alice told her.

'But why did she have to choose this way to do it? Did it bother her that much?'

Alice shook her head. A lot of answers came into her head, but none of them would have helped the situation.

'Is there anything else you wanted to ask?' Mr Carmody enquired, after a moment.

Jasmine's parents shook their heads.

'Thank you, Alice,' Mr Carmody said.

Alice knew that this was the signal for her to go, but she couldn't just turn and leave them like that. She had to say something. 'I'm really sorry,' she said at last.

It sounded so completely inadequate, but Jasmine's mother nodded at her and tried to smile. 'Thank you,' she said.

Not long afterwards, a police car came to take Jasmine's parents away again. From her seat by the window, Alice watched them go. She was glad they had not blamed her for what had happened and she wished she could have offered them some sort of explanation. But what could she have said? That their daughter had been stoned and in a slightly crazy mood? Or that she, herself, hadn't been paying attention to what Jasmine was doing because she'd been so busy getting off with a boy? That maybe Jasmine had been trying to prove something. Somehow. She could not have begun to explain any of this, so instead they had left as shocked and bewildered as when they had arrived.

At lunchtime, Mr Carmody stood up and addressed the students. 'I'm afraid I don't have any good news to give you,' he said, though nobody had really expected him to. 'It's been nearly twenty-four hours now and, as I'm sure you realise, in conditions like this the prospects are pretty hopeless. Of course, people have been known to survive at sea for extraordinarily long periods, even in very difficult conditions, and the search and rescue operation is still continuing but I'm afraid that we have to prepare ourselves for the worst.'

He paused after saying this, and there was complete silence in the room. Then he resumed. 'You'll be going home today, as planned. The coaches will be arriving in a couple of hours so, after you've eaten, I'd like you to go back to your dormitories and pack up all your belongings. I know it's hard to think about such things at a time like this, but it has to be done. First, please also make sure you have enough to eat. I know you may not feel like eating, but it's important at a time like this that everyone takes responsibility for his or her well-being and it would help us greatly to know that you're all prepared for the return journey. Thank you.'

He left the room, his head bowed and his back stooped. It seemed to Alice that the Mr Carmody who had started out on the journey from Beckerton, full of enthusiasm, with his snippets of information about every town or city they passed, was gone. The person who had taken his place looked and sounded like an old man.

Lunch was a dismal affair. The only sound from the diners was the scrape of knives and forks on plates as they sat in the gloom, each locked in his or her own thoughts. When they'd finished, Phoebe asked Alice if she was going to pack.

'You go on,' Alice told her, wanting to put it off for as long as possible. 'I'll be along in a little while.' She sat on in the dining room as the hostel staff went round wiping the tables and sweeping the floor. Eventually, however, she got to her feet and made her way to the dormitory.

Phoebe had already packed when she arrived. 'I'm finished,' she told Alice. 'Do you want any help?'

Alice shook her head. 'It won't take me long,' she said. But, as soon as Phoebe had gone, she realised that someone would have to pack Jasmine's clothes. This thought was so appalling that she sat down on the bed with her head in her hands while, one by one, the other girls finished their packing and left.

Once again, it was Ms Lucey who came and found her. She sat down gently beside Alice. 'Are you OK?' she asked.

Alice nodded. 'Someone's got to pack Jasmine's things,' she said.

'I know,' Ms Lucey told her. 'That's what I've come to do.'

Alice felt a huge sense of relief. She had been worried that they might ask her to do it and she was not sure she could have faced the task.

'I was going to wait until everyone had finished but I thought I'd better find out what had happened to you first,' Ms Lucey went on. 'Have you packed?'

Alice shook her head.

'Shall we make a start then?'

'OK.'

Ms Lucey got up off the bed and opened Alice's cupboard. She took out her clothes and handed them to Alice one by one. Automatically, Alice placed them in her rucksack. Soon the cupboard was empty and there was nothing left except Alice's birthday cards on the top and, beside them, the fossil. 'Are you going to take your cards?' Ms Lucey asked.

Alice nodded. She picked them up, but could not bear to look at them. Instead she put them carefully into her rucksack. Then she picked up the fossil and slipped it into her pocket.

'Right. I'm going to pack Jasmine's stuff now,' Ms Lucey said. 'You might like to go and join the others while I'm doing that.'

Alice nodded. She stood up and made her way out

of the dormitory, leaving Ms Lucey with the unenviable task of emptying out Jasmine's cupboard and putting everything away until there was nothing left to show that Jasmine had ever been there.

A little while later the coach arrived and they all climbed on board. Alice sat near the front and Phoebe came and sat next to her. Alice appreciated the gesture because she suspected that Phoebe would much rather have been with Adam. All the same, she didn't want to talk to anyone. She closed her eyes and tried to sleep. She found herself thinking about the conversation that she and Jasmine had had in the ruins of the old tin mine, when Jasmine had said that she'd wished she could be braver. If only Alice had said something more constructive at the time. Perhaps if she'd pointed out that being brave wasn't really so important, not as important as being alive, then Jasmine might not have felt the need to climb up on the wall and offer herself up to the waves like some kind of sacrifice.

She must have dozed for a while because the next thing she was aware of was somebody saying that they were leaving Cornwall. She opened her eyes and saw that they were indeed crossing the Tamar bridge. In a minute or two they would have left Jasmine behind in another county. It seemed like one last betrayal.

Seeing that Alice was awake, Phoebe turned to her. 'Do you think Jasmine had a premonition that it was going to happen?' she asked.

'What do you mean?'

'Well, she wrote that poem about drowning, didn't she?'

'Yes, but that doesn't mean she had a premonition.'

'Do you think it was just a coincidence, then?'

'Of course it was.'

'Some people don't think so.'

'Then they're wrong,' Alice told her. She felt angry with Phoebe for suggesting such a thing. It was like trying to romanticise what had happened, trying to make it into a story, when the truth was that it had just been a stupid accident that could so easily have been avoided. Unwilling to discuss it any further, she closed her eyes again and pretended to go back to sleep.

Nevertheless, she thought about what Phoebe had said. She could see how maybe it could look like that. But Jasmine had not expected to meet her death. The truth was that you never knew when tragedy would strike. You might think you were walking along a wide road and that you could see what was coming towards you. But all the time you were walking on a knife edge. The slightest mistake could send you hurtling off the edge.

She opened her eyes and looked around the coach. On the other side of the aisle, she could see Matt sitting next to Adam. In front of them, Gary was sitting by himself. The sight of him filled her with anger. *He* was the one who had brought the dope, *he* was the one whose idea it had been to go outside, *he* had come up with the suggestion of going down to the sea and *he* had been with Jasmine when the accident had happened. *He* had stood by while she climbed on top of the sea wall and then *he* had come running back to them in a panic when a wave had washed her out to sea. Afterwards, when the police had wanted to interview them, all he could think about was whether or not they would find out about the dope. When she thought about the way he had looked at her so beseechingly before her interview with the police, she utterly despised him.

The journey home seemed to take much longer than the outward journey. The traffic on the motorway was particularly bad. What with the delays and the number of stops they had to make at service stations, it was very late when they finally pulled up outside the school.

Alice's parents, like all the others, were waiting to meet her as soon as she stepped off the coach. Her mother put her arms around her and hugged her tightly. 'Oh, Alice. We're so glad to have you back!' she said. Then her father hugged her too. 'You poor thing,' her mother went on. 'It must have been so terrible for you.'

'I'm all right,' Alice said. 'Nothing happened to me.' She didn't want them fussing over her. It made her feel such a phoney. She was not the one who had fallen into the sea. She was not the one who had waved helplessly to the people standing behind the wall.

Her parents continued to offer their sympathy and reassurance as they drove home, but Alice said nothing. Her mother sat beside her on the back seat with her arm around her, but Alice felt stiff and cold and could find no answers to the questions they asked her about the accident.

'I don't understand what on Earth you were all doing going outside in the first place,' her father said.

Alice just shrugged.

'And why did Jasmine climb on top of the wall?' her mother wanted to know. 'She must have known it was incredibly dangerous.'

Alice shook her head. 'I don't really want to talk

about it,' she said.

'Of course you don't,' her mother said. 'Sorry, darling. We shouldn't be bothering you with all these questions. It's just what all the parents have been talking about non-stop. No one really understands what happened.'

Alice could just imagine them, standing around in a little group, waiting for the coach to arrive, swapping information. She knew she shouldn't blame them. They were only trying to make sense of what they had been told. But blame seemed to be the only thing that was left to her. Perhaps if she spread it around widely enough she could stop blaming herself so much.

When she got home, her parents insisted on treating her as if she was an invalid. Her father carried her rucksack into the house and then they made her sit down while her mother prepared something to eat. 'You look tired,' her father told her.

'I haven't been sleeping very well,' she admitted.

'Of course not. Still, at least you're at home now.'

But being at home didn't make her feel one bit better. She didn't know what to do with herself. She sat in an armchair staring in front of her like someone hypnotised. Her parents tried not to ask any more questions, but she could see that they really wanted to get to the bottom of what had happened. She understood their need to know but she could say nothing to help them. She'd already made up her mind about that on the coach home. There was no point in telling them about the dope, she'd decided. That would only freak them out even more. Nor would there be any point in mentioning what had happened between her and Matt. They would be shocked to find that their daughter had been busy kissing a boy while her best friend was being washed out to sea.

After she'd eaten, Alice went straight up to her room. She was about to get undressed when she noticed a photograph lying on the bedside cabinet. It was the one that had been taken during their trip on the London Eye. She sat down on the edge of the bed, picked up the photograph and studied it. From the midst of a group of happy tourists, Jasmine's scared face stared back at her. She looked about five years old. Alice opened a drawer and put the photograph away.

She had just climbed into bed when there was a knock on her bedroom door.

'Come in,' Alice said.

Her mother came into the room and sat down on the bed. 'How are you feeling now?' she asked.

'OK,' Alice replied. She thought about showing the photograph to her mother, but decided against it.

'You know you shouldn't try to hold it all in,' her mother said.

'I'm not.'

'Well, you haven't spoken about it very much.'

'I don't want to talk about it. It doesn't help.'

Her mother sighed. 'It's not good to bottle things up,' she said.

'There isn't anything to say though,' Alice insisted. 'It happened and there's nothing anyone can do about it.'

Her mother nodded, though it was clear that she didn't agree. 'Maybe it's a bit too soon,' she said. Then she bent down and kissed Alice on the cheek. 'Good night, darling.'

'Good night, Mum.'

That night, Alice dreamt that she was the one who was standing on top of the wall facing out to sea. The waves came crashing over her head. She felt a sudden shock as the cold water drenched her and then she was hurled off her feet and thrown into the sea. She struggled to stay above the water but it was no good. The weight of her wet clothes pulled her down and she sank like a stone. She knew that she had to hold her breath, but the prison of her lungs clamoured to be opened and at last she could bear it no longer. Desperate for air, she opened her mouth and breathed in water instead. She tried to cry out for help but no sound came. Instead she felt the iron grip of death tightening around her heart.

'It's all right, Alice.' Her mother was bending over her.

'What happened?' Alice asked.

'You were having a nightmare. We heard you shouting out.'

'Sorry. I didn't realise.'

'That's all right.' Her mother patted her on the head, as if she were a little girl. 'It's all over now. Do you want to talk about it?'

'I dreamt I was drowning.'

Her mother took her hand. 'You poor thing!' she said.

'I'm glad I woke up,' Alice said. 'What time is it?'

'Three o'clock.'

'I'd better go back to sleep. Sorry to get you up.'

'That's all right. Do you want me to stay with you until you drop off?'

'No thanks. I'll be all right now.'

'Are you sure?'

'I'm certain.'

Her mother kissed her on the forehead, then she

stood up. 'Shall I leave the light on?'

'No, you can turn it off,' Alice said. 'I'll be fine.' But, despite her assurances, she lay there for a long time after her mother had gone back to bed, recalling the horror of her dream and the terrible fear she had felt in the instant before death had claimed her.

It seemed like she'd only been asleep a matter of minutes when she was woken up again by the telephone ringing. She propped herself up in bed and looked at the clock on her dressing table. It was half past ten in the morning. But she didn't feel like getting up. She lay back down and closed her eyes again, ready to return to sleep, but a few minutes later there was a knock on her door and her mother came in. She sat down on the bed. 'That was Mr Carmody on the telephone,' she said.

'What did he want?'

Her mother hesitated.

Alice sat up in the bed. 'Tell me, Mum,' she demanded.

'They've found Jasmine's body.'

It was what she had expected, sooner or later, but to hear it put so bluntly was like being slapped in the face.

'She was discovered last night washed up on the beach,' her mother went on. 'Mr Carmody said he wanted you to be the first to know, after her parents of course.'

'Are they sure it's her?' Alice asked. The chances of there being some kind of mistake must have been incredibly small, but she wanted to be absolutely certain before she allowed the last faint glimmer of hope to fade away.

Her mother nodded. 'They found a travel card in her pocket with her name and photograph on it. I'm really sorry, Alice.'

Alice said nothing. She couldn't speak, she couldn't cry, she was totally numb as if she was in the middle of a vast empty space and everything else had been sucked out of existence, leaving her alone to contemplate this horrible truth.

Her mother took Alice's hands in hers. 'Can I get you anything?' she asked. 'A cup of tea or something?'

Alice shook her head. Nothing anyone said or did could possibly make the slightest difference to what had happened. They had found Jasmine's body, like a piece of litter that had been left behind. Jasmine herself had gone somewhere else, out of the world completely, and she was never coming back.

13

Going back to school on Monday was not easy. Alice was aware of the other students looking at her, whispering to each other as she walked past. She was conscious, too, of the teachers softening their voices whenever they spoke to her. She found it hard to talk to anyone and was aware that sometimes she seemed unfriendly, especially to Phoebe who must have been as devastated as she was, but who was still making an effort to talk to her. Of course, Phoebe didn't have herself to blame for what had happened. That was the difference.

Alice was not the only one who felt isolated. Gary and Matt also walked around surrounded by an aura of damage. And yet none of them spoke to each other. Whenever they were in the same room, Alice would be aware of Matt, his face showing very little emotion except for his eyes which were filled with pain. Occasionally she caught him staring at her but she always looked away again. Gary she tried to ignore completely, but it was impossible. She could not help noticing the way he sat hunched over, with his arms folded, like someone suffering from stomach pains, nor could she miss the nervous habit of blinking that he had developed. She knew she ought to feel sorry for him but she could not find any pity in her heart.

The school arranged for her to see a counsellor, a plump middle-aged woman in her mid-forties called Mary. Alice was nervous about going to see her at first and doubtful that talking to a stranger could help when she couldn't even speak to her friends or parents. But it was easier than she thought. Mary introduced herself and explained that everything Alice said would be confidential. Then she began by asking Alice how she felt about what had happened.

Alice thought about the question. There were so many different answers she could have given. She felt angry, sad and numb all at the same time. Some part of her still couldn't believe it had actually happened. But she didn't tell any of this to Mary. Instead she found herself saying, 'I feel like what happened was my fault.'

'How could it possibly be your fault?' Mary asked.

Alice explained about her and Matt. 'I wanted Jasmine to go away so that I could be alone with him,' she said.

'And do you really think that's why the accident happened?'

'No. But it could be part of the reason.'

Mary considered this. 'Are you saying that you believe Jasmine climbed onto the wall because she saw you kissing Matt?' she asked.

Alice shook her head. 'No. I just mean that I wanted her to go away and now...' She had been going to say, 'and now she's gone for good,' but she couldn't bring herself to say the words.

But Mary seemed to understand. 'We all have negative feelings about other people sometimes,' she said, 'even about people we love. That's perfectly natural and it doesn't make us responsible if something bad then happens to those people. Yes, you wanted Jasmine to go away, but you didn't want her to go away for ever, did you? And you didn't make it happen.'

'So why do I feel like I did?' Alice asked her.

'Because you're directing the pain you feel at yourself,' Mary said. 'That's understandable. It doesn't necessarily help, but it's what people do when they're faced with a tragedy like this. You look for someone to blame and the first person you find is yourself. It's a way of coping with what's happened.'

Alice would have liked to believe her but it seemed too easy, like letting herself off the hook. The truth was that she really was to blame. Herself, Gary and Matt. They were all to blame because they had allowed it to happen. If they had stayed inside the hostel, Jasmine would still have been alive. And nothing Mary said could convince her otherwise.

That afternoon Mr Carmody took Alice aside and told her that there was going to be an inquest into Jasmine's death. Alice was horrified. She hadn't expected this. 'Will I have to go?' she asked. The thought of standing up in front of a court and talking about what had happened was unbearable.

'I'm not sure yet,' Mr Carmody told her. 'I'll let you know as soon as I have any more information.'

She worried about the inquest for the rest of the day and that night she lay awake in bed imagining what it would be like. She had very little idea what would actually happen but she presumed it was like a law court and that she would be cross-examined by barristers who would demand to know exactly what had taken place on the afternoon in question.

But, to her great relief, Mr Carmody informed her the next day that she would not be required to attend the inquest in person. Instead, the police came to her house that evening and, with her parents looking on anxiously, took a written statement. Alice repeated what she'd already said so many times, that the four of them had decided to go out for a walk because they were bored, that they had separated into two groups, her and Matt and Jasmine and Gary, and that the first she had known of what had happened was when Gary had come running back along the path towards her.

The policewoman who was taking her statement wrote it all down without any comment, then she asked Alice to read it through and sign it. Alice's hand was shaking as she picked up the pen. There was so much that she had left out, and so much that could not be easily put into words. It made her feel like a fraud, like a criminal covering up some terrible crime.

Mr Carmody and Ms Lucey were both asked to attend the inquest in person and so was Gary, since he had been with Jasmine when the accident happened. They were all missing from school for three days. Alice did not envy them, particularly Gary. She thought of the questions he would have to face and she shuddered.

The verdict was reported on the evening news. Alice was in the living room with her parents when it came on. It was a shock. She'd assumed the media had lost interest in the story but here was a reporter standing outside a grey stone building somewhere in Cornwall, reminding viewers of how a sixteen-year-old girl on a school trip had been swept out to sea and drowned. They showed a photograph of Jasmine in her school uniform, obviously taken when she was much younger. Then the reporter informed them that the coroner had reached a verdict of 'death by misadventure'. Alice picked up the remote control and switched off the TV. She hated the way they spoke about it, as though it was just another news item, something to fill up space before they moved on to the weather forecast.

She had another counselling session the following day and when Mary began by asking her how she felt, Alice said, 'Angry.'

'Who do you feel angry with?' Mary asked.

'Everyone,' Alice said. It was true. She even felt angry with strangers she passed in the street because they could carry on with their lives, talking and laughing as if nothing bad had happened.

'So who do you feel most angry with?' Mary asked.

Alice thought about this. 'Gary,' she said.

'Because he was with her when it happened?'

'Yes. And because it was his idea to go outside…and because…' she hesitated.

'Because what?'

Alice hadn't intended to tell anyone about the dope after all, but she suddenly felt that it would be an enormous relief to talk about it. 'You won't tell anyone what I tell you?' she asked.

'Of course not,' Mary said. 'Everything that you say to me is entirely confidential. I've told you that.'

Alice nodded. 'OK,' she said. 'The thing is we'd had a spliff before we decided to go down to the sea. So we were all a bit stoned, I think, though I didn't even realise it at the time because I'd never smoked any dope before. But we were just acting a bit silly.'

'And you think this had something to do with Jasmine's death?'

'Well, I'm not saying it was the cause of it,' Alice said. 'I mean, the dope didn't suddenly turn us into different people. I just think we all got overexcited, you know, carried away, and maybe we did things we wouldn't have done otherwise. That's probably why Matt and I started kissing. I mean, we did want to and we would have done it at some time anyway, but I think the dope just sort of gave us a little nudge. Maybe the same thing was true with Jasmine.'

Mary nodded. 'So where does Gary come into this?' she asked.

'It was his dope.'

'Did he force you to smoke it?'

'Of course not.'

'So you could have refused, if you'd wanted to?'

'Well, obviously.'

'And so could Jasmine?'

'Yes, of course she could. Look, I'm not saying he made us do it. I'm saying that if he hadn't brought the dope, none of it might have happened.'

'We keep coming back to this, don't we?' Mary said. 'You keep saying that if something had been different, the accident might not have happened. But it did happen.'

'I know.'

'And blaming Gary isn't going to bring Jasmine back, any more than blaming yourself will.'

'I realise that,' Alice told her, 'but it makes me feel better.'

Mary raised one eyebrow. 'Are you sure about that?' she asked. 'Are you sure it doesn't make you feel worse?'

The funeral took place a few days later. The church was full of people, many of whom Alice did not recognise, but all the students in Alice's year were there and lots of the teachers. Across the aisle from her she saw Gary. He looked haggard and there were dark shadows under his eyes. She suspected that attending the inquest had taken its toll on him. A few rows in front of him was Matt. He, too, looked different – older, as if he had gone from being a boy to being a man overnight. Briefly, she wondered whether similar changes were written across her own face.

As she was thinking this, the congregation slowly began to rise to their feet and Alice realised that the undertakers were carrying in the coffin. She stood up with the others and watched the jerky procession make its way to the front of the church. She reminded herself that they were carrying Jasmine in the coffin and tried to imagine her friend's body lying inside the wooden box. But she still could not really believe it.

Then they all sat down again and the priest began to pray. From time to time the congregation joined in with the service, but Alice remained silent. Praying had not saved Jasmine, so why should she bother with it now? If there really was an afterlife, she thought to herself, then Jasmine was already in it, so what help would Alice's prayers be to her?

After a while, the priest finished praying, faced the people and began to speak about Jasmine's life. Alice didn't know how he could talk about her at all since, as far as she knew, he had never even met her. But she supposed that someone must have told him what to say because he told the congregation that Jasmine had been an enormously popular girl, the life and soul of every party. She had been loved by everyone who knew her and it was a shocking tragedy that she had been taken away from her family and friends so suddenly. But they were there today, he went on, to give thanks for her life as well as to mourn for her death.

'Whenever someone dies,' the priest said, speaking in a solemn, almost musical tone, 'they leave an empty space behind and we can never hope to fill that space again, nor should we try. But we can ask ourselves what it was that made the place they occupied in the world so unique, so special for each of us, and we can try to remember those special qualities, those gifts that Jasmine brought to everyone who knew her.'

Alice put her hand in her pocket as he said this and she felt the fossil that Jasmine had given her. She had been carrying it around ever since. She remembered how Jasmine had knelt beside her bed in the hostel and offered it to her and she felt the tears running down her face.

'We are, each of us, the sum of our memories,' the

priest went on. 'And we bring something away from every person we meet. Each one of us here today carries memories of Jasmine and we are the richer for that. So, although we cannot have her back here among us, let us give thanks for the time we knew her and cherish the memories she has given us.'

Afterwards, Alice went with her parents to the graveyard. That was the worst part of all. It was a bitingly cold day and she shivered as she stood with the other mourners watching the coffin being lowered into the grave. Finally the coffin bearers straightened up and stepped back. Then the priest dropped a handful of earth into the grave and it was all over. 'Jasmine is in the ground,' Alice thought to herself. 'I will never see her again.'

One by one, people went up to Jasmine's parents to commiserate with them. Alice hung back, reluctant to face them, but Jasmine's mother caught sight of her and came over. 'Alice,' she said. 'It's good to see you.'

It was the first time that Alice had faced her since the day they had spoken in the office of the hostel. 'I'm so sorry,' Alice said.

Jasmine's mother's eyes were red from weeping but somehow she managed to smile at Alice. Then she put her arms around her. 'You were a good friend to Jasmine,' she said. 'She was always so happy to see you.'

Alice could not speak. That Jasmine's mother could be so generous astonished her. If it was me, she thought, I would probably hate all of Jasmine's friends for leading her into danger – instead she has put her arms around me.

Other people were waiting their turn to talk to Jasmine's mother, so Alice said goodbye and moved away. As she did so, she noticed Gary at the edge of the crowd. He was looking in her direction and blinking rapidly like someone who has just emerged into the light from a darkened room. She suddenly felt desperately sorry for him. He had always been so sure of himself, but would never be like that again. Perhaps her counsellor was right. Perhaps blame was not the answer. She thought about the prayer she'd said on that terrible night while the rescue teams had searched the waves for Jasmine's body. She'd promised to be a better person, if only Jasmine would be found alive. Her prayer had not been answered. But maybe she could still fulfil her side of the bargain. Maybe she could try to be a better person. Wasn't that something she owed to Jasmine? She made up her mind and walked over to Gary. She took a deep breath. 'Hello,' she said.

He looked startled and smiled nervously. 'Hello, Alice,' he replied.

That was all they said. Then they turned and walked away in different directions, but afterwards Alice was glad she had spoken to him.

The following day Matt came up to her after school and walked alongside her as she made her way to the bus stop. 'I hear you spoke to Gary,' he said.

'I just said "hello",' Alice told him. 'It was no big deal.'

'It was to Gary,' Matt said. 'He's been having a pretty bad time.'

'I'm not surprised.'

'Don't be too hard on him. He's changed a lot,' Matt told her.

'We all have,' she said. 'You know what I was thinking about just before you came along?'

'What?'

'That time when we were in the pub in Belmouth and Gary told me I needed to grow up.'

Matt nodded. 'Yeah, I remember.'

'Well, I think I've grown up now.'

They had reached the bus stop and Alice stopped. 'This is where I get my bus,' she told him.

'I know,' Matt said, 'but there was something else I wanted to ask you.'

'What?'

'Remember when you said that none of us were behaving sensibly on that night?'

Alice thought about it. She vaguely remembered the conversation. 'What about it?'

'Do you regret what you and I did, kissing, I mean?'

She studied his face. She was used to thinking of him as someone who was very self-sufficient, someone for whom other people's opinions did not particularly matter, but he was looking so earnestly at her now that she suddenly saw how vulnerable he was. She thought about what he had asked her. Did she regret what they had done?

Finally Alice shook her head. 'No, Matt,' she said. 'I just wish it had happened at another time.'

Matt nodded. 'So do I.' He hesitated. Then he said, 'Would you like to do it again sometime?'

She reached out her hand and put her finger to his lips. 'I'm not ready for anything like that right now,' she told him.

'But you might be in the future?'

'I might be,' she said. After all, life had to carry on. She smiled at him sadly. 'Thanks for asking.'

'That's OK,' he told her. 'See you around, Alice.'

'Yeah. See you around, Matt.'

He stood there for a moment longer, as if he was thinking of saying something else. Then he turned and walked away, leaving her standing by the bus stop with the ghost of a smile still playing around her lips.

The young woman continues to stare out at the water which is the colour of beaten metal, while the little girl beside her stands and watches. Then, after a moment, the young woman raises her hand and very faintly waves.

'Who are you waving to, Mummy?' the little girl asks.

Her mother looks at her absent-mindedly. 'I was waving to a mermaid,' she replies at last.

The little girl looks at her mother open-mouthed and wide-eyed. 'Are there really mermaids out there, Mummy?' she says.

'Yes, there are,' her mother says, taking from her pocket a smooth black stone with a fossil at its heart. 'See this. It's a mermaid's earring.'

The little girl takes the stone and examines it carefully. Then she turns back to her mother. 'Can I keep it?' she asks.

Her mother nods. 'But you have to promise to look after it very carefully,' she says.

'I promise,' the little girl says solemnly.

The young woman puts out her hand. 'OK then, Jasmine,' she says, 'let's go home now.'

ALSO BY BRIAN KEANEY

1 84121 437 X   £4.99

BALLOON HOUSE

When Neve was a child, her father used to make up special stories for her about the magic Balloon House. But it's hard to recapture this intimacy now that he's moved away and remarried. Neve is determined not to like her father's new family. But then danger explodes into Neve's life, calling on her deeper feelings of love and loyalty. Trust in her father and their shared memories may be the only way to survive.

'Thoughtful and exciting.'   *Books for Keeps*

1 84121 005 6 £4.99

BITTER FRUIT

Rebecca's dad is always moaning. One night Rebecca has had enough. She tells him she hates him. And these are the last words she will ever say to him. Grief at her father's death is mixed with terrible guilt. And while Rebecca is trying to cope with these powerful emotions she discovers that her father had a terrible secret, and suddenly life becomes unbearably complicated. Now Rebecca must learn to face tragedy...and the truth.

'A gripping read.'   *Sugar*

SHORTLISTED FOR THE NORTH EAST BOOK AWARD AND THE SOUTH LANARKSHIRE BOOK AWARD

1 84121 858 8   £4.99

FALLING FOR JOSHUA

Abi knows there's something special about Josh
the moment his deep blue eyes meet hers. But
Abi has a secret. And she's so used to keeping it
hidden that she can't trust him. She's been
rejected before. But one night something terrible
happens and Abi's secret is revealed. Will Josh
stand by her, and will Abi learn to accept the way
she is?

'An ideal book for teenage readers.'
                              Times Educational Supplement

1 84121 530 9   £4.99

FAMILY SECRETS

Kate's mother, Anne, has a past full of secrets.
Why did she leave her home in Ireland before
Kate was born? Why does she never speak to
Kate's grandmother? And why does she never
mention Kate's father? Now Anne and Kate are
making the long journey back to the west coast of
Ireland where Kate's grandmother is seriously ill
in hospital. Will Kate find out about her father
and solve the mystery of her mother's silence?

1 84121 758 1   £4.99

WOLF SUMMER

BY ANDREW MATTHEWS

'Anna? I'd like you to meet Pete.' Anna turned, and her breath was taken away. Pete was beautful.

Pete's gorgeous, but unfriendly. Anyway, Anna's got other things on her mind. Sent away for the summer to stop her seeing her boyfriend, Anna is pining for her lost love. At first. But then she gets involved in the local wolf sanctuary, and discovers a dangerous passion. A passion that eventually throws her and Pete together in a time of crisis.

'A great holiday read all about young love, teen angst, funky grannies and wolves. What more d'ya need?'   *MIZZ*

1 84121 831 6   £4.99

GET A LIFE

BY JEAN URE

Joel's brother, Noah, is a real heart-throb, always dating different girls. But when Lars Kennedy turns up things seem to change. Tall, blond and gorgeous, everyone falls for Lars! Then comes a startling revelation. One that will have fatal consequences..but will also be the start of a new life.

'Clear and sensitive, direct and fair.'
Times Educational Supplement

'It'll pull on those heartstrings. What are you waiting for?'
MIZZ

MORE ORCHARD BLACK APPLES

❏ *Balloon House*	Brian Keaney	1 84121 437 X	£4.99
❏ *Bitter Fruit*	Brian Keaney	1 84121 005 6	£4.99
❏ *Falling for Joshua*	Brian Keaney	1 84121 858 8	£4.99
❏ *Family Secrets*	Brian Keaney	1 84121 530 9	£4.99
❏ *The Private Life of Georgia Brown*	Brian Keaney	1 84121 528 7	£4.99
❏ *No Way Back*	Linda Newbery	1 84121 582 1	£4.99
❏ *Break Time*	Linda Newbery	1 84121 584 8	£4.99
❏ *Windfall*	Linda Newbery	1 84121 586 4	£4.99
❏ *Get A Life*	Jean Ure	1 84121 831 6	£4.99
❏ *Just Sixteen*	Jean Ure	1 84121 453 1	£4.99
❏ *Wolf Summer*	Andrew Matthews	1 84121 758 1	£4.99

Orchard Black Apples are available from all good bookshops,
or can be ordered direct from the publisher:
Orchard Books, PO BOX 29, Douglas IM99 1BQ
Credit card orders please telephone 01624 836000
or fax 01624 837033
or e-mail: bookshop@enterprise.net for details.

To order please quote title, author and ISBN
and your full name and address.
Cheques and postal orders should be made payable to 'Bookpost plc.'
Postage and packing is FREE within the UK
(overseas customers should add £1.00 per book).

Prices and availability are subject to change.